SURRENDERED CONTROL

A CONTROL SERIES NOVEL

Anna Edwards

Cover Design by www.CharityHendry.com
Logo Design by Charity Hendry
Book Layout © 2015 BookDesignTemplates.com
Editing by Dayna Hart, Hart to Heart Edits
Formatting by Charity Hendry

Surrendered Control/ Anna Edwards -- 1st ed.
ISBN 978-1539380917

Dedication and Acknowledgements:

To Charity.... I can never repay your kindness.

The biggest acknowledgement for getting this book published has to go to Charity Hendry. She gave me the confidence to find my voice and write and then she guided me through the whole process and was always there when I wobbled. She is also responsible for the fantastic artwork. I cannot thank her enough. So to my twin from another country, I love you to bits and thank you so very much.

I would also like to thank my editor Dayna Hart. She has polished this book to what it is that you will read today and I have definitely learned a lot from her patience and understanding. I also want to thank my friend John for his initial read through and the subsequent ones.

I also want to thank my beta readers, Angela, AJ, Kris, Maggie, Jenni and Mary. Your thoughts and discussions as you all read the book really helped bring it to life.

Finally, I want to thank my family for all their support both financially, emotionally and in babysitting duties just so that I can write. I especially want to thank my husband for giving me a chance to achieve a dream. I love you so much.

CONTENTS

CHAPTER ONE

Amy

The full moonlight glistened over the endless volcanic sand as Amy emerged from the water. The bright illumination shone on her honey-blonde hair and she brushed her fingers through it. The day of travelling had left her tired and the warm water had eased her aching muscles, cramped by the budget flight. This was her first holiday for many years. Aspiring writers didn't tend to have the money to travel. Nor dancers in a gentlemen's club, forced to work just to make ends meet. But it wasn't as bad a job as it sounded; she was well protected, as her uncle ran it and made sure she was sheltered from the seedier side of the profession. And she enjoyed the dancing side, in fact, it was her second passion. Her uncle Stephen had paid for this holiday to Lanzarote as a twenty-first birthday present. Ever since her parents had died in a car crash two years ago, he had always looked out for her. He was the only family she had left, and she looked up to him and trusted him implicitly.

As Amy took a towel and wrapped it around her body, the aroma of the freshly caught fish being cooked was everywhere and made her mouth water in anticipation. She decided on a small tavern that was filled with more locals than tourists. Amy wasn't big on the mass-market tourism of the island--she preferred places of culture and history--but as the holiday was a gift, she couldn't refuse it. She ordered the grilled catch of the day with salad, and a glass of the local *La Geria* wine. As she watched the sun slowly set over the shimmering waves, the tension in her shoulders began to dissipate.

When she had finished her delicious meal, Amy ordered

another glass of wine and pulled out a little notebook from her bag to begin writing down some of the details of the island so far. She liked to bring her personal experiences into her writing, and she wanted to get everything noted should it be needed for future stories.

She had just finished a passage on the chaotic wait for her luggage at the airport when an uneasy tingling warmed her skin as though she was being watched. Looking up, she met the alluring sky blue eyes of a man sitting across the room. Had he just arrived? Or how had she not noticed him previously? He too was sitting alone with just a glass of wine for company. Upon making eye-contact, Amy couldn't help but blush. He was exquisitely handsome. He had a rugged yet smart look, a defined jaw line, and short dark hair that he ran his fingers through as he watched her. The top few buttons of his blue linen shirt were undone and revealed a muscular upper body that oozed a primal masculinity. His stare was intense, and she felt herself being drawn into it even more. When his lip twitched at her blatantly checking him out she pushed the other chair at her table out with her gladiator-sandaled foot and looked up, smiling at him with a cheeky grin that masked her excitement. For a moment, she thought he wasn't going to move, but then he got to his feet. Even the way he walked was sexy, she was glad she was sitting down as her legs felt like jelly at his presence. He took a seat and held his hand up to the waiter, who promptly took his order for a more expensive bottle of wine. Neither of them spoke at first, they just continued to take each other in.

"James." His voice was deep and inviting, and she was pleased to note he was speaking English.

"Amy." Her voice was smooth and possibly a little bit too sexy when she spoke.

Silence.

"Well, if this isn't awkward." He ruffled his hands through his hair again. The bottle of wine arrived, and the waiter poured them each a glass.

"Shall we start again? I'm Amy, I'm twenty-one, I come from London, and this is my first holiday in a while. I have come away to finish writing my first novel."

"I am James, I am twenty-eight. I also come from London, well Kent initially. I haven't had a holiday myself for a while. I tend to be a workaholic."

"What do you do?"

"I work in property. It is all very boring, I am sure you don't want to hear about it. So; a novel. Is it all hush-hush or can you tell me something about it?" He sat back in the chair, his left leg resting over his right, the wine glass tantalisingly resting at his full lips. Lips that she couldn't tear her eyes away from. She wondered what they would taste of if she kissed him? He seemed happier to be asking questions than answering them so she decided to answer him to continue that line of conversation.

Amy chuckled and took a mouthful of her wine. "It is a classic. Boy meets girl, boy loses the girl, boy wins the girl back forever."

"Interesting. So this boy? What is he like?"

"Tall, dark, and handsome."

James nodded with genuine interest.

"And the girl?"

"Pretty, slim."

"Blonde?"

"Blonde."

"I like this story already."

"Told you it was a classic."

"Certainly is." He raised his eyebrow as he spoke. "So, is the man proficient in the bedroom?"

"That is a little presumptuous isn't it?"

"Why?" He chuckled now as he refilled the glasscs they both seemed to have drunk rather quickly.

"They have only just met."

He shrugged, "Why should they waste time, if there is an attraction between them?" James reached forward, took Amy's hand, and their eyes met in an intense stare as sparks of electricity flowed through them both. She wasn't drunk, so it wasn't that. "Are you staying nearby?"

The question hung thickly in the air between them.

Amy had had only one previous partner, and that was a boyfriend of four years. Strange as it seemed she felt she knew James, which was odd since they had only set eyes on each other not fifteen minutes before. "Yes, the Rivera apartments."

"Do you want me to walk you home?"

She didn't doubt from the look on his face that this would turn to sex if he did. But something about him, something about the mystery of his tone prevented her from saying no. He had a presence about him that drew her under his spell.

"Yes."

James pulled out his wallet and put forty euros on the table. The walk back was short, and they talked a little more. Just general facts, where they grew up, favourite foods, drinks, and a particularly funny story about an encounter that he had had with a flock of seagulls in Brighton. Amy didn't tell him she worked in a Gentleman's Club.

When they entered her apartment, she was suddenly nervous. James took a seat on the cream sofa, and Amy went to look in the kitchen for a drink. She found two glasses and a semi-chilled bottle of wine and returned to the lounge. His big body was so commanding in the small lounge.

"Sorry, it isn't more. I only arrived today."

"It is fine. I still haven't bought any wine for my apartment so you are a step ahead of me."

"How long have you been here."

"A week now. A few days left. How long are you here?"

"Only a week."

"Not long to finish that novel then."

"No. Not really. I will have to forgo sunbathing and do lots of writing."

Amy put the bottle down on the table; she needed a corkscrew to open it. "I won't be a minute. Just have to figure out which drawer the corkscrew is in." She turned back to walk into the kitchen but stopped as James called out 'Wait'. It was the way he said it -- it sent shivers of anticipation down her spine. Slowly she turned and looked at him, her eyes wide. He had risen from the sofa and was walking towards her.

"Take your dress off."

"I...."

"Take your dress off, Amy."

She had no answer. Her mind was telling her this was crazy, but her body was doing as he asked, completely disobeying the part that was telling her to tell him to fuck off. She reached down to the hem of her dress and pulled it over her head. Amy wasn't big breasted so, underneath the summer dress, she hadn't worn a bra. She stood in front of him in just a pair of white lace panties. He walked around her, studying her, taking in every inch of her prickling flesh. She could feel the heat of his gaze marking her. Amy was never *naked* in front of the clients at the club, but she wore revealing clothing, and none of that could prepare her for what she was feeling right now. He leaned over her and took a deep breath, he was smelling her.

"You are beautiful." His tone was calm but had a stern undercurrent to it.

"I was supposed to be getting you wine."

James laughed. "I am going to kiss you now. Are you sure you want to do this?"

"I don't think I would be standing in front of you in just my panties if I didn't. Now are you going to remove some of your clothing?"

"Eager. I like it. But we will do this my way." James pulled his shirt over his head, and Amy noted she was indeed correct about his superbly toned chest. She couldn't see his back, but she saw on his left arm he had a tattoo. It looked like the tips of wings.

"What is your tattoo?"

His face went momentarily blank. He didn't answer but pressed his body closer to hers. He leaned in and kissed her. Tender at first, and then with intense passion. Amy could feel her knees weakening as she was pushed back against the wall. "Place your hands above you head and don't move them." Again with the authoritative tone.

"Why?"

"Will you do as I asked, Amy? Or should I leave now? I told you, we will do this my way. You will enjoy it. Don't worry." A hot kiss was again pressed to her lips and without thinking anymore, Amy moved her hands above her head. "Good girl. You will be rewarded for that later."

Rewarded? James moved his mouth from her lips down to the peaking tips of her nipples. His tongue swirled around the sensitive buds and she let out a yearning moan. He looked up at her, a mischievous look in his eyes and began to travel down the flat line of her stomach until he knelt on the floor in front of her. He placed his hands on either side of her panties, and in one fluid motion ripped them from her body. Amy was breathing fast now. This whole experience was so damn intense it almost seemed like a dream, her body was on fire, and she longed for him to touch her.

James put his hands between her legs and parted them to reveal her neatly trimmed sex. He groaned. "I haven't even touched you yet, and you are ready for me. Have you been like this all night? I can even smell your arousal."

Amy sure as hell wasn't going to let him know that he was turning her on more than she ever had been before. "You know how to kiss a lady and get her excited. It is a good start, just depends on what skills you have now."

He gave her a little tap on the top of her thigh which brought a scream from her and then ran a finger over her displayed folds before moving it slowly into her inner channel which was already slick with the need for him.

"If you doubt my skills again, I will put you over my

knee." Amy's body writhed against his hand as she found herself being excited about having her bottom spanked.

Holy hell. Where had that come from?

His thumb found the hidden bundle of nerves between her thighs and teased it. She could feel the heat within her starting to build. "If you don't stop doing that, I am going to come all over your hand." James abruptly withdrew his finger and got to his feet with a tutting sound.

"No. Not yet. You will come when I tell you that you can." He looked her in the eyes, and it was almost like he was controlling her body with his words.

"You are not in charge of me you know that right?"

He didn't answer, only sniggered, reached into the pocket of his trousers, brought out his wallet, and retrieved a condom from it. The wallet was then tossed aside, and Amy watched as he lowered his trousers and pants to reveal a substantially thick cock and covered it with the condom. It was jutting up towards his stomach and was a work of art. It should be framed and hung in an art gallery it was that perfect. She was panting now; she was terrified that the length and girth of his manhood was going to hurt, but at the same time she needed him buried deep inside her. She wanted to know what he felt like. Amy pulled her hands down and reached out to touch the muscular sinews of James' shoulders.

"No. You don't touch me unless I give you permission." He slammed her hands back against the wall and held them there with one hand. With the other, he lifted her leg from the floor and in one slow thrust pushed inside her.

"Oh God." Amy groaned. He was nothing like she had felt before. Her ex-boyfriend wasn't small, but sex between them had always been something that they seemed to do because they were boyfriend and girlfriend. This was different. It was raw, and it was dangerous. James began to move slowly. Their eyes locked together as with each long movement he stroked against the sweet spot deep within her.

Their lips tangled in a tumultuous tango of passion. James' hand still held her in place, and she was glad for it because she was barely able to support her weight as she felt the build-up of her climax again. She tried to suppress the feeling. James had told her that she couldn't come until he had told her she could, and she wanted to please him.

Jesus, what was this man doing to her? This was her body. Why was it responding to his control like this?

James seemed to know she was close and trying to control herself; she could tell by the little curl of his lip. She wanted to hit him. She wished he would let her release. He finally let her out of her misery when he leaned forward and collected her lip between his teeth. He nodded consent, and Amy exploded around him. Wave after wave of cataclysmic pleasure rolled over her shaking body. She called out and James joined her over the precipice as he released himself into her.

They were both covered in sweat, breathing rapidly, their legs quivering. James lowered her leg to the floor and withdrew from her, checking the filled condom as he did.

"Are you alright? I didn't hurt you, did I?" Amy shook her head; she couldn't find her voice just yet. "Good." He pressed another kiss to her now-bruised lips and looked into her eyes. At that moment, something within him changed. Amy saw it. Gone was the dominantly splendid lover he had been; he withdrew into himself. He pulled up his trousers, quickly found his shirt, and put it on. "I am sorry. I shouldn't have done that." And with that, he left Amy confused, standing naked, covered with the scent of the best sex she had ever had, and her hands still above her head.

CHAPTER TWO

James

James could still smell her scent, no matter how many times he showered. She had gotten under his skin. Why had he walked out? He cursed himself for being such a fucking idiot. He could have been with her again and again, and he grew hard just at the thought.

But he could never be normal. He could feel the tattoo burning on his back, the permanent reminder of what he was. So why did he continually torture himself?

Sitting in his office, overlooking London, he angrily swiped the paperwork in front of him to the floor and walked to his safe, opened it, and took out a file.

It hadn't taken Matthew, his bodyguard, long to find Amy's details. He was ex-MI5, after all.

James read the words on the cover sheet again:

STRICTLY CONFIDENTIAL,
"Amy Jones, D.O.B. 25th January 1996. Brentwood, Essex.

Only child of Gavin and Judy Jones: both deceased 14th October 2012.

Resident in Kennington, London, SE11. Purchased April 2013.

He then returned the file to the safe and locked it.

He couldn't do this anymore. He already regretted having Amy's details. He had a meeting and needed to concentrate on that. It was just a holiday fling. If she saw him again, after the way he had left her, she would probably slap him in the face. He gathered his papers and headed to the boardroom. His secretary flicked her hair as he passed.

She clearly had a thing for him, which he was starting to find irritating.

"Marie, can you ask Simon to have the figures on the Argentinian project on my desk in the next half hour, and could you also tell him to stop flirting with the girls in Accounts if he wants to keep his job?"

"Of course, sir. I will see to it at once" she called after him, but he barely heard her. He was lost in the memory of Amy.

Amy

Amy pulled the collar of her thick coat up around her ears as she emerged from the Kennington tube station. It had been difficult to keep warm since her return home. She had acquired a beautiful tan but was unable to show it off in the miserable February weather.

The final few days in Lanzarote had been occupied by a flurry of writing. She had managed to nearly finish her novel, but she couldn't help but feel disappointed with it.

When she had returned home from the holiday, she put her computer in a drawer and vowed not to look at it for at least a couple of weeks. Until then, she would immerse herself in her dancing, perhaps seek some overtime, and try to forget about both her writing and her brief encounter with James. Although that was going to be hard, given how often she'd been replaying the events of that evening in her mind. Why had he been able to control her that way? How had he done those things to her body? And why did he disappear? What did she do wrong?'

When she entered the club, Amy's uncle greeted her with a warm embrace. "Hello, little kitten. You have fun in the sun?" he kissed both her cheeks and then stood back looking proudly at her.

'Kitten' had been her nickname since she was just four years old. She had been given a cuddly toy cat from her parents as a birthday present, which she carried everywhere as a young child, and to this day she still owned it. It now sat on top of the wardrobe in her bedroom, albeit in a slightly worse for wear condition, with just one eye and half a tail.

Amy hesitated, blushed, and then responded. "It was lovely uncle Stephen. Thank you so much. It was ever so generous of you."

"I'm pleased" he said. But then his familiarity changed to a business-like demeanour. "Sara has called in sick" he moaned; "I'll need you to dance on both stages tonight, and you'll only get a fifteen-minute break between." He chuckled and gestured to her tummy. "But I'm sure you ate and drank far too much in Lanzarote so it will do you good."

Amy hadn't actually put on any weight whilst away. She'd been very careful with what she had eaten. She didn't mention anything, however, and just giggled. Her uncle always liked to have the last word. "Of course, uncle Stephen, Not a problem. I'll go get ready now."

He was already walking away from her towards his office as he called back, "Good girl. I knew I could rely on you"

Amy shrugged off her heavy coat, and headed towards her changing room that she shared with Sara. They had been friends ever since she started working at the club. Sara was a few years older than Amy, and had been there for almost a decade. She had an Amazonian look, with jet black hair and big sultry eyes. She was stunningly beautiful and was much sought-after by the punters in the club; a fact she often used to her advantage in generating additional income. For not only did the club provide public dancing, it also offered private lap dancing in the backrooms. Not that she would consent to doing any of these despite how much her uncle complained about it.

Amy couldn't recall a time Sara had taken a day off sick. Worried that something could be wrong, she quickly took her mobile from her bag, texted her to check how she was, and offered to drop around at the end of her shift.

As Amy sat down at her dressing table to apply her makeup, she could see the freckles on her face and shoulders, which always appeared upon her spending any time in the sun. Although she was supposed to wear thick makeup, she decided that tonight she was going to opt for a more natural look, and applied just a little dab of blue eye shadow, a fine amount of black eyeliner and a touch of long-lash mascara. Amy had a gentle wave to her strawberry-blonde hair. She decided to leave it down, giving her a bohemian appearance. She selected a studded bodice with a short jagged-edged silk skirt from the wardrobe and after putting them on, she slipped on her favourite pair of small silver heels. She was feeling a sense of anticipation and excitement to be returning to the dance stage that she had been away from for almost a fortnight. She loved to dance. It was a shame she didn't have any training and could actually do something like theatre work with it. All she had was dancing for drunken men. There had to be something more to her life than this.

James

When he arrived home later that evening, James went straight for a workout and then a shower. He stood in his large shower, resting his head against the wall of his ensuite bathroom. He had managed to put Amy out of his mind for the last few hours. The scorching water ran over his powerful shoulders and down his defined masculine chest and lean waist.

Grabbing a towel from the rail, he dried his dripping body, put on a pair of black jeans and a blue linen shirt and headed to the kitchen.

His mother lived with him, although she had her own floor in his large Kensington house. She helped with the housekeeping and looked after the place whilst he was away. James kissed her on the cheek as she handed him a chilled bottle of beer from the fridge.

"Did you have a good day at work?" she asked him with a devoted smile.

James nodded, "Did you speak to Sophie?" he asked.

"Yes, she has finally chosen the navy gowns."

His sister was getting married and was being a bit of a bridezilla. At twenty-three, she was five years younger than James and he adored and protected her, as he did his mother.

James approved of her fiancé, even though the pair of them were rather wayward, likely to just fly through life on a soft breeze and see where it took them. James had insisted on paying for most of the wedding. Sophie didn't need to accept as her fiancé was a millionaire in his own right, but she knew how much it meant to James to be able to provide this for his sister given their father was totally out of their lives. He had left under an extremely black cloud a few years previously. His mother placed the plate of food in front of him and wondered off to her room leaving James alone with his thoughts.

Just as James was finishing his dinner, his bodyguard entered, looking rather pensive.

"Evening. Is everything alright?"

"Um, yep. Oh, your secretary said that Enquirer has been on the phone again, asking about the interview for their magazine."

"They don't take no for an answer, do they? Perhaps I should just agree to it. At least it would get them off my back." While he accepted the media's focus on his business affairs, he liked to keep his private life just that.

"I'll have to protect you from even more female attention if you agree to it. I'm not sure how I'll cope." Matthew chuckled as he sat down with his food.

After a short silence James asked, "So, did you follow her?"

Matthew nodded.

"Is it safe?" he asked.

This time, he shook his head and frowned.

James dropped his knife and fork to clatter on his plate as his heart missed a beat.

"It's a gentlemen's club. Run by her uncle, a Mister Stephen Jones."

Matthew also put his cutlery down.

"What does she do there? Waitressing? Bar-work?"

"No boss, She's a dancer. An erotic pole dancer. But from what I could establish, that's all she does." He took a deep breath and continued. "Her uncle though...." Matthew reached into the pocket of his suit jacket and handed James his phone with a video on it. James pressed play and clenched his jaw.

"Is she is there now?" he asked.

"Yes, boss."

"Give me ten minutes." How could she be so stupid? Or was he the stupid one? Did she know who he was? Was she playing him? "Matthew, we are going in hard. Make preparations."

CHAPTER THREE

Amy

When it was Amy's time to dance, Mrs Barton, the stage manager, called at her door.

"There is a full crowd out there tonight. Make sure you dance well, Amy. Could get a few decent tips." The middle-aged woman peered behind the curtain. "If you would remove a bit more clothing you would earn a fortune."

"My act is more about the illusion of sexuality, Mrs Barton. It works better with my clothes on."

"Well suit your bloody self. More money for the other girls, then."

"As long as I have enough at the end of the week to cover my living costs, I'm happy."

The first half of Amy's set went well, although during it she felt strange. Like all the hairs on her body were standing on end and a heat flooded through her body. She put the feeling to the back of her mind, tucked her tips into the bra part of her corset, and headed to the bar to get some water and take her short break.

The club was heaving. It was a Friday night and the city traders were celebrating the end of the week. One of them, looking totally inebriated, staggered into her slurring as he spoke. "Care to give me a private dance, darling?"

"I never kiss on a first meeting," she said. "Now, how about you go find your friends."

He groaned and staggered backward, struggling to stand up properly, as a security guard approached and then escorted him unceremoniously away. She looked over to where she knew her uncle would be sitting. She smiled cheekily at him, as if to say she had matters completely under control, and he winked back.

When she finally made it to the bar, the barman presented her a glass of water with ice and a squeeze of lemon. He knew what she liked.

"Thank you, Pierre." she said, blowing him a playful kiss, and he dramatically bowed.

"You are welcome Miss Amy. How was the holiday?"

"Hot, wet, and relaxing."

"Sounds like a typical day in here without the relaxing bit." The barman chuckled and Amy joined in.

"You ever wanted something more than this, Pierre?"

"What, like waiting in a high class joint?"

"No, a different job. Do you have a dream?"

"Nobody can make as good a Manhattan as me."

"You are right there. Save me one for later."

"You are not paid to talk and flirt, Pierre. I believe you have people waiting for drinks." Pierre instantly turned and served another patron.

Amy turned toward the voice. "Hello Leon."

"Aren't you supposed to be working as well?"

"I'm on my break."

Leon was one of her uncle's 'henchmen'. He was also a total slimeball.

"I think your break is about to finish. Unless you want to come and share some of it with me. I know a room that is free. You can show me how much you missed me."

"Well, that won't take long. I didn't think of you once while I was away."

"One day, you will beg for me to stick my cock in your tight little cunt."

Amy stepped off her stool and headed back to the stage. "In your dreams, Leon."

James

As they entered the club, James and Matthew showed their I.D. The bouncers and girls on the door were experienced in recognising wealthy clients, and they were both quickly offered a private booth. A bottle of Dom Perignon was shortly brought to the table by a scantily-clad brunette, who was followed by a smartly-dressed man who introduced himself as a senior member of the management team and requested they ask for any services they may require.

James looked around trying to locate Amy. It took him a few moments and a double take before he realised that the girl dancing on the back stage was her.

God she looked sexy. The seductive, swaying movements of her curves were intensely erotic; if he touched himself, he would have exploded in an instant.

"You better drink this, boss." Matthew said handing James his glass from the table.

James drained it.

James was impressed as he saw Amy deal with a drunk, closely observing as a bouncer then escorted him away. James followed Amy's gaze as she smiled at a man who was clearly her uncle and the owner of the establishment. She seemed to think her uncle had sent the bouncer over. In fact, he was paying no attention to the fact that she could have been molested in the middle of the club.

"Have them bring the uncle over," James said to Matthew.

Amy's uncle didn't take long to arrive at the table. He was greying at the temples, had a slightly portly figure, and his features were harsh. James saw nothing of Amy's warmth or kindness in his eyes. To be polite, James got to his feet and reluctantly held out his hand.

"Mr North. It is a great pleasure to welcome you to my club. Please, anything we can do to make your visit more pleasant, don't hesitate to ask. "

"Thank you Mr Jones. The blonde with the wavy hair who was dancing earlier." He pointed to the second stage. "I'd like to meet her, privately." James reached for a neatly bound collection of fifty pound notes and placed them on the table. "And I am willing to pay ten grand for the privilege."

Amy

Amy went to the other stage to check everything was in order for her second act. A fifteen-minute gap gave her no time to relax. She would be exhausted when she got home.

At the curtain, waiting to commence her second set, Mrs Barton reappeared.

"Change of plan, Amy. Your uncle wants you."

"What is it?"

"He wouldn't tell me. He says he will tell you himself."

Amy sighed, and rushed over to her uncle.

"Mrs Barton said you wanted me?"

"Amy, with Sara off tonight, I need a favour from you. We have an important guest asking for a private dance, and all the other girls are busy."

"But what about the stage? There will be no one on it?"

"Mrs Barton is going to shift some of the curtains around, and Jenny will dance for both crowds."

"So why can't I dance for both crowds and Jenny do the private dance? uncle, please. You know that I don't like the private dances. Don't make me do it."

"Don't argue about this, Amy" her uncle replied sternly. "Just do as you are asked. The club is full tonight, and I have a lot to do."

Amy looked down forlornly, reached out, and tenderly touched his hand. She was so ungrateful sometimes. He was trying his hardest to look after her, and she was fighting him. What would one dance hurt?

"I'm sorry uncle Stephen. Of course I will do it. Which room do I need to go to?"

"Number One" he replied, looking slightly calmer.

Amy quickly went back to her dressing room and freshened up a little. A quick squirt of some perfume always seemed to heighten their senses and made the inevitable 'coming in their pants' happen quicker.

The next thing she knew she was standing outside of the private room with the client waiting inside. She took a deep breath, checked her clothing was in place, and opened the door. The room was darker than normal, almost pitch black. With a little unease, she stepped forward and closed the door behind her. She couldn't hear anything. From the centre of the room came a deep breath, followed by a long, drawn-out sigh that sent shivers down her spine. As a single soft light turned on, she heard a voice she never thought she would hear again. "Hello, Amy."

"James," Amy gasped.

CHAPTER FOUR

Amy

Amy trembled as James slowly stood. He had the same intensity that he had had before but this time, she sensed anger in him.

"How did you find me?"

He snapped back with a curl of his lip, "Chance" he said sarcastically. "This wasn't the sort of place I expected to find you in. I thought you were innocent. Shows what I know."

"I didn't think I would see you again after you walked out." Amy replied. "Did you have to get back to your wife?" Who did he think he was?

The man who had given her the best orgasm of her life was in her place of work and insinuating she was a whore. He would have obviously paid to get her alone in this room. What a bastard.

She was furious that he thought he could just show up here after walking out on her the way he did with no explanation and expect her to submit to him the way she had then. She switched on her business manner. He was not going to control her this time.

"If you would return to your seat Sir, I will begin the dance you have paid for. First, though, I would like to remind you that you are not to remove your hands from the side cushions during the dance, and you are certainly not to touch me at any point.

James didn't stop advancing on her.

"Sir, sit down."

"No." Amy wasn't scared -- there were cameras in the room and her uncle would be having them watched. If James didn't stop, she would only have to make a signal and a bouncer would be in to protect her. She composed herself with a deep breath.

"Take a seat please, sir, or I will call Security to have you removed from the premises."

"Answer me one thing, what do you do here?"

"I dance. Why?"

"Just dance?"

"Yes."

"And this?" He pointed to the chair where she would give him the lap dance.

"If I can avoid it, I do. My friend is sick tonight." He winced at the mention of her friend. Why?

"Are there cameras in here?"

"Yes?" She motioned toward one. "What is going on?"

"My name is James North. I am a billionaire, and I can buy whatever I want. I paid ten thousand pounds for my time with you."

"Time with me?" Amy's world was collapsing in on her. "Do you mean...?"

"I won't touch you." James interrupted her, though. "But I have to tell you something. Please sit. I need you to listen to me."

Amy's damn body betrayed her mind again, and she instantly sat down on the chair. James came and perched on his haunches before her.

"Your friend who is off sick. What have you been told?"

"Nothing, my uncle just mentioned she was ill."

"She isn't sick. She is... injured."

"Injured?"

"She was violently assaulted by your uncle and several of his men."

"What?" Amy laughed, was he insane? Her uncle wouldn't do something like that. "I don't believe you."

"Amy, please, you have to listen to me."

"No, I don't. I don't even know you. You fucked me and left me. Why should I trust you?"

"You shouldn't, but I need you to. We have to leave

here, now."

"You're mad." Amy pushed him away, ran to the door, pulled it open and was faced with her uncle.

"Mike, Dave, take her back in the room and hold her down if necessary so Mr North can conclude his business. It is about time she faced the reality of what actually happens in this club. I am no longer willing to support this spoilt and naive little bitch."

Amy stood there in shock. She couldn't believe what she was hearing. This man was her flesh and blood; he was the only family that she had, and he was condoning and even assisting in rape.

The two bouncers grabbed her arms tightly and dragged her into the corner of the room, with James, and her uncle watching. Another man she didn't know appeared at her uncle's side.

Amy lay helpless on the floor, looking up at the four men.

Then, in what seemed like an instant, James threw the back of his elbow into one of the bouncer's faces knocking him to ground, as the other man who she hadn't seen before delivered a flooring punch to another bouncer. What in God's name was going on?

James knelt beside her, removing his jacket and trying to place it around her shoulders. She scrambled to her feet and backed away from him, still looking petrified.

James stood back up and turned to her uncle, "Miss Jones will be resigning with immediate effect. You will see to it that a good severance pay is prepared for her, which my bodyguard here will collect from you tomorrow. You try and contact Amy again, and I will kill you."

Her furious uncle decided to take a swing at James but was held back by the bodyguard.

James turned again to Amy offering her his hand but again she shuddered and stepped back.

"Amy" he pleaded, looking tenderly at her. "Amy, please, listen to me. This was all horrible but necessary to reveal the exact nature of your uncle and what goes on in this club I am sorry, but he is not the man you thought he was. He has so many secrets." He pulled his phone from his pocket and pressed the play button.

Sara appeared on the screen. She looked terrified, backed up against a wall. Her voice echoed out of the phone, pleading for mercy, but all Amy could do was watch as Leon and several other men rained down punches on her body. When they stepped back, Sara lay unmoving on the floor. All that Amy knew shattered when her uncle walked over and kicked Amy's friend in the stomach. Amy let out a cry as the video stopped. Tears started to stream down her cheeks. He was the man who she thought had protected her. The man who had looked after her since her parents had died. Standing up, Amy swallowed hard, formed a fist, and sent it flying into the face of her uncle. She followed it up with another and another. She was screaming and crying.

Strong arms circled her waist to pull her away. She swung round and landed a punch on James as well.

She had to get out. She ran. Behind her, she could hear James calling for her to stop, and her uncle calling for additional security.

The cold night air was like a slap in the face. She stood in the alleyway next to the club wearing virtually nothing; crying and shaking. What was she doing? Where could she go? Should she go to the police? She stumbled towards the main street. Everything was a blur, but she could tell that people were staring at her. She could hear their exclamations and disgust at her appearance. Nobody tried to help her. Why would they? For all they knew, she was a drugged up prostitute.

She heard footsteps running up behind her and turned to lash out again, but she stopped when she looked into James's eyes. Here was the lover who had brought her to blissful levels. The man that she knew, she could trust, even after one brief encounter.

She sank to the cold pavement, exhausted and freezing.

He put his coat over her shoulders and brought her into his arms. He took her bloodied hand and gently kissed it. Part of her wanted to pull away from him again. Her head was spinning as she tried to take everything in.

"I am sorry Amy. There is so much I need to tell you. But not now. We need to get you somewhere safe and warm." A car pulled up beside them. "Amy this is my car, and my bodyguard, Matthew, is driving it. You are safe. Please get in the car. I promise I won't hurt you. I am going to take you back to my home. My mother is there." He held out his phone. "If you want to speak to her the entire time we are driving you may."

Amy just looked blankly at him.

"I don't know," Amy said shaking her head. She looked at the car and the concerned look on the driver's face, and then back to James.

"You have my word no harm will come to you while you are under my protection." He waved his phone at her. "Here take this." He unlocked it, and she took it. "Google my name. James North. You will see that in there I gave you the correct details about myself." Amy pulled the phone close to her and did so. It brought up pictures of him and details of the company he owned. She just flicked through it, as he watched her. "You know exactly who I am now. If I hurt you in any way, you can go straight to the police."

Amy stood up, and James helped her into the car. She turned to him. "I am trusting you, James. Please don't let me down."

CHAPTER FIVE

James

James could feel himself shaking as he slid into the black leather car seat beside Amy. He reached over her fasten her seat belt, and she flinched again. He wanted to hold her, but even if she never allowed him near her again, at least she would now be away from her uncle.

Amy turned and looked at him as though he was a monster. Maybe he was. Her eyes were as wide as saucers.

"How?" Her voice wavered as she spoke.

"How what?" he said calmly.

"How did you know where I was? It wasn't chance, was it?"

He shook his head and turned away from her. "The day after I got back from Lanzarote I asked Matthew..." —he shifted his look in the direction of the driver— "...to find out as much about you as possible."

"Why?"

"I don't know. We had a one-night stand. It was marvellous. Well, it was for me. I wanted to know more about you. Maybe meet you again."

"So you could destroy the only life I know?"

The comment felt like a stab to the heart, and he had no reply. They sat in silence for the rest of the short journey.

As he helped her out of the car to the front door, he could see the astonishment on Amy's face. She turned to him,

"You own this?"

He nodded and she faltered again at the top step.

"You won't force me?"

James stuttered over his answer; her heart-rending pleas were breaking him.

"I promise you, Amy."

He opened the door, and his mother came rushing down the stairs towards them. Matthew had warned her.

"Get her upstairs. You poor thing, you must be half frozen. Let's get you inside. I have the fire on and have made a nice cup of tea for you. How do you like it? Milk? Sugar? You are safe now. Come on you poor thing."

James watched as his mother direct Amy towards the blazing open fire. She sat her down on the cream leather sofa and placed a hot tea on a small table beside it.   Tea was his mother's solution to everything.

"James, find Amy something warmer to wear. Your sister must have something here that will fit her. Something nice and comfortable, mind you. Try and find some pyjamas." He nodded. Before he disappeared down the corridor he turned and gave a final look to Amy. She was watching him. Even after everything he had done, he could see she did still trust him.

It didn't take James long to find clothes for Amy to wear, and as he went back into the lounge he saw Matthew had joined them, sitting in his favourite chair with a fine cognac.

"I hope you poured one of them for me too."

Amy fixed her eyes on James as he spoke. "Amy, I know mum says that tea cures everything, but I think we all sometimes need something a little stronger."

Matthew slowly got to his feet and with a sarcastic bow went to pour two more glasses.

"I have put the clothes in the guest bedroom next to mine. Mum, would you mind showing Amy to the room?"

She nodded and helped Amy to her feet. Amy continued to watch James, and he didn't need to look at her to tell. He felt the deep scrutiny of her gaze.

James sat down in his large brown antique leather chair, suddenly exhausted. Matthew returned with the cognac and handed it to him. He drank it down in one long mouthful. It burnt his throat with its rawness but it was what he needed.

"You alright boss?"

He looked up at Matthew and smiled. "Just about. Thank you for everything tonight Matthew. You know, I would be lost without your help."

"Now a good time to ask for a pay-raise?"

James just raised an eyebrow.

"Worth a shot." Matthew said as he sat down again, and both men sat in silent contemplation for a moment.

"What happens with Miss Jones now?"

James shrugged his shoulders and slouched down into his seat, "I guess that will depend. But I can tell you; she is not going back to that club under any circumstance. She will be staying here for the week at least. I want to check out where she lives first thing tomorrow to make sure it is safe. I suspect she left belongings at the club as well. I want you to get them when you collect her severance package tomorrow."

"Do you think her uncle will give up on her that easily?"

"I want her tailed every second of the day. Hire whoever you need. I don't want her out of their sight unless she is safe with me or here in this building."

"You going to tell her that you are having her followed?"

"No."

"Boss, if you are hoping to have a relationship with her, then surely you need to be honest."

"Not yet. I need to get to know her first. I need to know she will accept me the way I am, especially if I turn..." He abruptly paused as Amy walked back into the room. She looked even sexier in the low-swung pyjama bottoms and tight-fighting top. He could see her erect nipples pushing through the fabric. The look in her eyes told him every-thing; they had renewed sparkle as she took the seat on the sofa again and tucked her legs up underneath her. James passed her the cognac Matthew had placed on the table.

"It will help you sleep." He looked at the clock; it was one in the morning, but he was far from tired. His mum yawned. "Go to bed, mum. You are tired. I will show Amy your room if she needs you."

His mum looked to Amy, and after a quick look to James for reassurance, Amy responded. "Please Mrs North, you go to bed. You have been so kind to me. I will drink this and probably go myself."

"If you are sure."

"I am." His mother got to her feet and held her hand out for him to kiss before she walked down the corridor to her part of the house whilst James indicated to Amy where his mother's bedroom was situated.

"I have a couple of errands to run before bed, so I will bid you goodnight as well." Mathew said smiling at Amy, "It is lovely to have met you, Miss Jones. If there is anything you want during your stay here, just ask."

Amy looked a little puzzled, "My stay? I will go home, tomorrow, first thing. I need to find a new job."

"You have had a big shock, Amy. Why don't you consider staying here as my guest for a few days? We have a pool and a gym in the basement you can use."

"Am I a prisoner here?"

"Of course not. You' d be free to come and go as you please" He got up from his chair and sat next to her on the sofa. She didn't flinch but defensively crossed her arms. "Amy, I am sorry. I promise I will explain everything. But not tonight. You need to sleep. What you have been through today will have left you shaken and greatly confused. If you wish to return to your apartment tomorrow, I will take you myself, but please consider my offer. I know I have no right, but I would like to get to know you better."

She stared at him. He could see she was weighing everything up in her head, going through all that had happened. She then slowly nodded her head.

"I will stay until the end of the weekend. Three nights. But I need to return home tomorrow to collect some clothes. It isn't right, me wearing your sister's." She sighed heavily, "And I will need to go to the club. My bag, phone, and keys are there.

"I will send Matthew first thing in the morning to retrieve them. I am sorry, but you can't go back there"

"You don't control me, James. I will do what I want."

"Amy. It's for your safety. Please trust me."

"Tomorrow, I want you to tell me exactly what is going on. I want you tell me everything you know about my uncle"

"I promise you, Amy. I will tell you everything."

She got to her feet. " Goodnight James."

"Goodnight Amy."

James switched the TV on low and began to flick through the channels. Amy was in the bedroom next to his, and she was hurting. He was going to have to explain to her why he walked out on her in Lanzarote. He just wanted to bury himself inside her to make it all right, but that was where all his problems had started.

His hand reached down and undid his trousers. He pulled his cock out and began to stroke it. He shut his eyes and thought of Amy in the costume she had been wearing in the club. He remembered the scent of her as they had had sex in Lanzarote. The little cry she made as she came. He was gripping really hard now, and roughly tugging at his throbbing shaft. He was going to come, he needed to come, but at the last minute he pulled his hand away. That was his punishment.

He would never be worthy of her.

CHAPTER SIX

Amy

A shaft of light shone through a small crack in the curtains. Amy slowly opened her bleary eyes and looked around the unfamiliar room. Expensive-looking tapestries decorated the pristine white walls. A large mirror sat atop an ornately-carved wooden dressing table and a matching wardrobe was on the other side of the room. She reached for her phone on the bedside table to check the time, but it was not there. As she rolled over, her body ached and she remembered the night before.

She pulled the bedcovers over her head and screamed loudly into them.

She was alone.

She slowly got out of the bed and pulled on a dressing gown that had been left on the back of the door. A hairbrush was on the dressing table and she quickly pulled it through her hair. She looked at her reflection in the mirror and saw dark circles under her eyes. She still didn't know what the time was, and so she quietly opened the bedroom door and peered out. The house was silent. She remembered her way to the lounge and went to see the time. It was eleven A.M. She'd slept for much longer than she had thought.

A voice made her jump, but as she turned and realised it was James' mother, she relaxed.

"Good morning, Mrs North."

"Amy, please, will you call me Miranda? Come, I have some breakfast, well brunch by now I would think, in the kitchen. You must be famished."

She was. She followed Miranda into the kitchen, where laid before her was an assortment of pastries, fresh fruit and on the stove were sausages and bacon. The smell of freshly ground coffee permeated the room.

Amy looked around the room for signs that James had woken and had his breakfast.

"James left early. Urgent business meeting apparently. He said he will be back as soon as possible and for you to relax, take a bath, swim, watch TV, to do whatever you want, and he will take you to get your belongings later."

Amy sat at a large table and Miranda poured her coffee.

"He seems a very busy man. Is that how he became so successful?"

Miranda busied herself at the massive stove as she answered,

"He works more hours than I care for him to do. The holiday he took recently was his first in about five years and I am sure he was constantly on his phone and laptop whilst there."

"He seemed relaxed and happy. He certainly didn't have a laptop with him." Amy blushed as she realised the implication of what she had said. "I mean when we had dinner."

Miranda served Amy her cooked breakfast and sat beside her, "It is alright dear, I am not daft. It was obvious to me that something had happened between you both."

Amy cut a piece of the toast and egg and popped it in her mouth. It was delicious and she swallowed it down hungrily before going back for more.

"He scared me last night, and I still don't fully understand why he acted the way he did. But I can see he is a good man. I see the way he treats you. I would like to get to know him." The words had come out of her mouth before she could think about what she had said. She was still angry with James, but she wanted to understand him. She was intrigued by his intensity and wanted to peel back his layers to discover what was beneath.

"I am glad of that." Miranda smiled as she topped up Amy's coffee.

Amy surveyed Miranda as she took her empty plate. She

was slim, smartly dressed, and held herself well. Her hair and nails were clearly attended to professionally on a regular basis. She looked like she was in her mid- to late-forties, but with a twenty-eight-year-old son, Amy suspected she may be a little older.

" I am just going to see what clothes Sophie has that can you wear."

Amy called after her as she headed out of the kitchen, "Is Sophie his sister?"

Miranda called back. "Yes. Help yourself to another pastry. Nobody leaves my kitchen hungry."

Amy chose a ripe apple from the fruit bowl, and a phone vibrated on the counter. She looked and saw the message was from James to his mother. She knew she shouldn't, but she then read the brief notification header.

It is all trashed. Keep Amy there.

Amy read the message again, before it disappeared. Trashed? What had been trashed. She grabbed the phone and sped through the house calling for Miranda, who appeared quickly from another bedroom with clothes in her hand.

Amy held her phone up to her. "Where is James?"

The elder lady snatched it from Amy, "What did you see?"

"Where is James?" Amy shouted.

"Amy calm down, please. Sit down." Amy stood. "He went with Matthew to get your belongings from the club. Your uncle wasn't there. James was told he was at your apartment." She looked down at her phone and pressed her finger against it to unlock it. Amy didn't need to hear the rest.

"He's destroyed it, hasn't he? I need to go."

"Amy, James said you need to stay here. It is not safe--"

"Isn't safe? It's my apartment." Amy grabbed the clothes and stormed along the corridor to her room. "I'm going with or without your help. I'll walk the entire way if I need to."

The traffic was light so it only took Miranda half an hour to drive them to Amy's apartment in Kennington. Amy got out of the car and sped up the six flights of stairs to her door. The door was slightly ajar and she nervously pushed it open. A vintage mirror--a Christmas gift to herself--was shattered in front of her. Further down the hallway, an array of ripped furnishings and smashed ornaments were scattered over the floor. This was her first home, these were her possessions, and they had been completely ruined. She heard a noise from the lounge and as she entered, she saw James and Matthew carefully trying to pick up pieces of furniture. Her stereo system and TV had been smashed. The sofa had been cut and its filling pulled out. Her eyes focused on an empty picture frame on the floor. It was the one that contained the last ever photo that had been taken of her with her parents. It was now torn into tiny pieces scattered beside the frame. It could never be replaced.

She let out a loud sob and James turned. "Amy. What are you doing here?"

He let go of his half of the coffee table, much to Matthew's anguish when he had to balance it himself, and wrapped his arms around her. Amy didn't shy away. She needed the comfort. "You were supposed to stay with my mum." Miranda appeared at the door now.

"Amy." He cupped her cheek, his piercing blue eyes trying to calm her obvious distress. "Let my mum take you back to my place. Matthew and I will sort everything here."

Amy leant further back into his warmth. "Is every room the same?"

"Yes. I am sorry."

"Why did he do this? I don't understand."

"I don't know, Amy. But he will pay for it."

"You have called the police?"

"No. The police will do nothing. He had your keys, they will view it just as a domestic." Amy knew what James meant by he will pay, for now, she was too raw with anger to argue.

"I had my mum's jewellery in my bedroom." James let go of Amy's waist, took her hand, and led her to the bedroom. Matthew and Miranda stayed in the lounge and continued cleaning. Amy went straight to her jewellery box, which was thrown on the floor. Relieved to find her mum's wedding and engagement rings there, she placed them on her fingers.

"I need to get the police involved. Without a crime reference, I won't be able to get my insurance to fix and replace everything." She pulled her hand through her hair in desperation and looked back at James. The look of concern had gone from his face. He had the look of determination and control again. The one from that night.

"You won't need money. I will sort everything."

Amy interrupted, "James, I am not going to let you repair everything at your expense."

"I won't be repairing anything at my expense."

"My uncle won't be repairing this either. I want him gone from my life, James. After what he did? I want to forget him."

"I will deal with your uncle my way, but you won't be returning here."

Amy wanted to defy him, to scream at him and tell him no, but she couldn't. She didn't want to stay here. He was overruling her common sense again, but she had fallen completely under his spell. She looked away at the pile of all her clothes, her intimate undergarments that were strewn all over the floor.

"I agree. On some conditions."

"You have a thing for conditions, Amy. We will need to work on that."

Amy turned back to him and took a kiss from his lips that shocked them both.

"I'll pay my way. You won't keep me."

James raised an eyebrow, "We can negotiate that." Amy

laughed. "The other conditions?"

"Just one."

"I am all ears." He put his arm round her waist again.

"Whatever this is between us, it won't last if we don't get to know each other properly. No lies. No secrets. You messed up last night James. You should have come to me and told me everything, not made a public display of it. This..." -- she waved her hands at the chaos of the room -- "is partly your fault."

"And I will never stop apologizing for it. It is why I want to help you correct it. It is why I am here cleaning it myself."

"I was a little surprised at that. I thought you would hire someone. But, James, if you accept my conditions, I will stay with you and take your help. If not, leave now." Amy brought her finger to her lip and nervously chewed on the tip as she waited for his answer.

James placed both his hands around her waist.

"I agree."

CHAPTER SEVEN

James

It didn't take them long to finish packing what remained of Amy's belongings. A locksmith had arrived and changed the locks while they were there. He went to hand Amy the key to lock up, but she just shook her head and told him to give them to James.

She didn't seem to really have much fight left in her. The past twenty-four hours had been too much for her, and he felt overwhelming guilt for his part in it. James had allowed his controlling nature to overrule his common sense –again-- and Amy had suffered as a result.

He helped her out of his mother's Audi after they had parked and then he carried one of the suitcases into his home. Amy carried the lighter of the two; not that either was heavy.

Amy went straight to her room. James thought she needed a moment alone and went to make them some drinks. When he returned, Amy was hanging up her final dress. She looked up at him, pleading. "I want you to tell me everything."

He took both of her hands and pulled her close. She kissed him gently on the lips. She tasted so good. Why couldn't he just take her away somewhere and make her forget everything that was happening, instead? He really didn't want to see her crying.

"I trust that you did it for the right reasons, James. I am still so confused by my uncle. He is not the man I grew up believing him to be. I need to know everything to get it all straight in my head."

James took her hand and in silence lead her to his study on the top floor of the house. Most of the Georgian house was in keeping with the period, but it had modern twists. This room was no exception. He had a massive, curved oak desk in the middle of it. To the right on the wall, he had three large screens which could be hidden under pictures that descended from the ceiling.

James showed Amy into the room and sat her on velvety chaise longue. He went to a safe, which was again hidden behind a picture, and pulled out a folder. He handed it to Amy.

"This is everything I found out about you."

He felt ashamed by the file as she took it from him. That folder contained so much personal information about her. If she put the folder down and walked out on him now, he wouldn't blame her; it made him look like a stalker. However, she just flicked through all that information and stopped at the details he had on her uncle's business.

James knew that her uncle used the premises as a front for drugs and prostitution. He imported girls from Eastern Europe with the promise of a brighter future only to have them carry out sex acts in a property he owned nearby. Amy wiped a tear from her eye.

"I thought Sara got some of her extra money from... selling her body. I didn't know he had another property that did all that. Those poor girls."

"Matthew and I will be working to shut that part of the business down."

"Let me know when you have."

Amy turned over another page and looked up at James in shock.,

"Sara?"

He nodded. "Sara isn't her real name. She is Gabriella Martinez. She's from Latin America. Amy, did you know she was your uncle's lover?"

"James, she can't have been. We used to complain about him together. I never thought she liked him but that she tolerated him because I was his niece and she earned good money."

"The video I showed you was from a week ago, when you were in Lanzarote. It is security footage from the club. Matthew had someone hack into the systems. She was pregnant with your uncle's child. He didn't want it, though. Amy, the only reason your uncle paid for your holiday was so that he could get you out of the way while he got rid of the baby." He handed her back the papers but turned to a page which had photos of Sara's body after Amy's uncle had enacted his cruel termination on her. Amy's hand flew to her face and she paled.

"Yesterday, Matthew found Sara in her apartment. She had taken an overdose of painkillers. She didn't survive." Amy let out a loud cry that almost tore James' heart apart. He wanted to lash out. He wanted to punish her uncle for the pain he was inflicting on Amy.

For now, though, he needed to concentrate on the girl he cradled in comfort. She sat up, and he wiped away the tears from her eyes. "That is why I came for you straight away. I wasn't thinking straight when I heard about her death. I had to get you away and protect you."

"She has no family?"

"Matthew found her family. We are arranging to get her home to Brazil. Amy, Sara was duped by your uncle. There were letters and a diary in her flat which showed that she thought he would marry her. She was a good girl and took her life as a last resort because she felt so much shame."

"Thank you for returning her home." Her voice broke. "How can he have done that to her? To make someone think that death is preferable to life? I should have been here to help her."

"Your uncle is a sick man. He is perverted and danger-ous, and there is nothing that you could've done. Please let me protect you from him?"

She pushed him away and stood up.

"You must be crazy getting involved with me. I should go. It isn't fair to you."

He frowned but didn't move.

"You are going nowhere. As you said earlier, we have a connection and we owe it to ourselves to explore it. Come here."

She instantly obeyed him.

"You are safe, and we can learn about each other now. Trust me. If I didn't want to do something, I wouldn't. Sara made a mistake and paid with her life."

He didn't finish what he was saying as she crushed a passionate kiss to his lips. He reciprocated at first and then pushed her away.

"James, I need to feel something other than the pain. I need to be back in Lanzarote."

James froze. He wanted nothing more than to tear her clothes from her and bury his aching cock deep within her. But she was vulnerable at the moment.

"Lay back." His tone was stern, and she immediately did as instructed. He pulled the trousers she was wearing down her legs and then ripped her thin panties from her body. "Open your legs."

She did so, revealing her already-glistening pussy to him. He leaned forward to trail his tongue over the length of her folds, parting them, and savouring her juices. He was throbbing with his own need. He flicked his tongue over and over her clit, and every time she groaned in pleasure. Slowly he inserted a finger inside her, then two; and she thrust herself against his hand. His finger hooked, he teased her g-spot. She was close. He stopped, and she moaned.

"Not until I say, Amy, remember? That is my rule."

She cried out. "And you complain about me with rules and stipulations."

With his free hand, he gave her two quick sharp smacks to her peachy rear.

"Answering back gets you into trouble."

"James please."

"James, please what?"

Breathlessly, she clutched at her perfectly formed breasts and gyrated against his hand. "Please, let me come."

He chuckled. "Come."

James flicked the nub with his tongue and she exploded. She gushed over his tongue and gripped his fingers in pulsating waves of ecstasy. He longed to bury himself inside her, but as she came, her tears flowed. She sobbed. He moved to cradle her, and held her close.

CHAPTER EIGHT

Amy

A month had passed since Amy had moved into James' home. She was enjoying learning more about him and had made wonderful friends in both Matthew and Miranda. Two days after her laptop had been smashed, James presented her with a brand new MacBook Pro with a variety of writing software installed and all her work she thought lost neatly stored in what he called a 'cloud'. He had given her a new iPhone as well, and she was told that it was linked to his account so she could download anything that she wanted on it. Her contacts were all on it, minus her uncle. Amy didn't complain, she made a mental note to pay him back one day but enjoyed the modern technology, even if it baffled her a little bit. He had also had pictures of her with her parents recovered from her laptop and printed out and put in frames in her room. She had bawled like a little girl when she had seen them. They had also spent a lot of time together just having what James termed dates.

Today was one of those dates, and he was taking her shopping. Matthew pulled the car into Sloane Street and all Amy could see was top designer brands.

"James, I can't afford to shop here. In case you forgot I don't have a job."

"I can buy you a present."

"No. Please, can we go somewhere cheaper? I don't want you having to buy me expensive clothes. You seem to think that it is just one outfit that I need. Most of my clothes were destroyed, I pretty much need everything."

"Then I will buy it for you."

Amy groaned and placed her head in her hands.

"You are not listening to me. I am not going to let you

buy me everything."

"I have the money, I can spend it however I want, and I want to spend it in these shops." He had that defiant look on his face that told Amy he wasn't going to listen.

"Fine." Amy leant forward and spoke to Matthew. "Matthew, James is getting out here to spend his money. Can you take me to Oxford Street please so I can spend mine?"

"What. No that isn't what I meant" James spluttered next to her. "Matthew you stay here."

"If Matthew stays here, then I am not getting out of the car. You can, but I won't move a single muscle from this seat."

"Er, boss? Sorry, but I need a decision as to what I am doing. A traffic officer is heading this way."

Amy folded her arms over her chest and sat back in her seat.

"Fine. Take us to Oxford Street. But I will be buying your entire wardrobe."

"You will buy me one outfit, and you won't argue. I am adamant, and you won't change my mind. I am not here for your money. I am here for you."

"I think we need to have a long discussion about defiance, and soon." James shrunk over to his side of the car, and Amy was confident that he was sulking. He had the whole stuck out bottom lip thing. She was secretly cheered by her little victory even though she knew it would mean punishment later. James was very skilled with his fingers and tongue, and if she denied him something, he denied her. He always relented in the end, normally when she begged. He had kept to his word and not pressured her into anything more even though she could see he was very evidently hard every time he touched her.

The rest of the date passed with very little event.

But when she returned home she found a Mulberry Bayswater handbag waiting for her. She didn't protest, even after she had Googled the cost. She liked it and thought he had made an excellent choice. He had promised her a Chanel one next and she told him that there was no way he was to buy her one. She would take it straight back to the store.

"Have you decided what you are doing with your flat?" James asked as he poured her a glass of Prosecco.

"Well as you won't let me pay you back for all the repairs I thought that I would rent it out."

"Not sell it?"

"I don't have a mortgage on it, so renting it out will give me some money of my own 'til I find another job."

"You don't need a job."

"Don't start, James. I am finding a job."

"Why? I am a billionaire. And when we open the hotel in Bangalore I will make more money than I know what to do with. Let me spoil you?"

Amy wasn't going to get anywhere with James in this mood. He wanted to treat her like a princess and protect her, but she could never live her life that way. It was how she had been treated by her parents and her uncle and where had that got her? No, she needed to stand on her own two feet.

"Tell me how you made your business so successful. Where did you grow up?"

"Changing the subject won't help you win the argument, you know." He looked at her with a raised eyebrow. "But I will indulge you this once. My parents came from Kent. They had some money so I went to grammar school and passed all my GCSE's and A-levels with top grades but I didn't go to university despite being offered a place at Cambridge."

"Why?" Amy interrupted.

"I didn't want to. I had other plans. I had a trust fund, and when I received it, I brought a plot of land at auction. With a few trusted builders and a trainee architect, I developed three houses on the land and sold them at a triple profit. We just went onwards and upwards from there."

"Do you still use the architect?"

"He is a shareholder and chief architect of the company.

The head builder is head of my operations team."

"Their loyalty to you paid off, and vice versa."

"Certainly did. I had wanted my sister to work with us as well but after dad left us she wanted to forge her own way in life. I may have greased the wheels a little bit for her to do that but please don't ever tell her so."

"You really adore Sophie don't you?"

"I do. I still can't believe she is getting married. Did you like speaking to her the other day?"

"I did. She teased me something rotten about you though." Amy snuggled further into James' arms. She shut her eyes and listened to his heartbeat.

"What did she say? I will have words with her."

"She was laughing at you for, finally, at your ripe old age of twenty-eight, finding a girlfriend."

"That's it. She can pay for her own wedding."

"You wouldn't dare."

"Try me."

"She did say something that worried me a little bit. She mentioned that when the press finds out about us, they'll want to do interviews."

"They probably will, but we will deal with that when it happens. Maybe I will give them the topless photo shoot they keep asking for, and they will leave you alone."

"I am not sure I like that."

"Getting protective over my body Miss Jones?"

"Maybe a little. I love your tattoo. I caught a glimpse of it when you were changing the other day. Why a male angel? It is so intricate."

Amy was confident that she felt his heart skip several beats and started rapidly thumping as she asked the question.

"I saw the design and liked it. Do you want another drink?"

"No, I still have some of this one." Alright, so he wasn't going to talk about his tattoo. Every time she tried to get him to open up about something that wasn't his business or his family he shut down. She wasn't going to allow it to happen this time.

"James, am I your first proper girlfriend? Is that why the press will be so interested in us?"

He groaned. "Shall we watch a film?"

"Stop avoiding the question."

"Stop *asking* the question, and I will stop having to avoid it."

Amy sat up. "James, please. Why do you always avoid this question? You know everything about my past love life."

"Yes, I do, and I wish I could erase the thought of another man touching you."

"Is that why you won't talk to me about your sex life? Because you think I won't like the thought of you with another woman?"

"Amy."

"No, James. If we are to have a relationship, then we need to be open with each other. You can't keep secrets from me." She raised an eyebrow at him as she sat up.

"You are not going to stop are you?"

She shook her head.

"Alright, I give in. I have had a proper girlfriend; I met her when I was sixteen. We were together for five years. Yes, we had sex, before you ask. No, it wasn't as good as my one encounter with you." He smirked. "Now, shall we watch a film or do you want to question me more?"

"Why did you break up?"

He got up from the chair and ran his hand through his hair. "We wanted different things from the relationship."

"She wanted marriage?"

"No."

"You wantcd marriage?"

"No."

"Then what?"

"We were sexually incompatible Amy."

He drowned his glass of Prosecco and turned his back to

her.

"Incompatible?"

"I have certain needs. I am controlling, you know that already, but I also like certain things sexually."

"Oh. So...you are into whips and chains? She wasn't submissive but you think I will be."

"You already are Amy, whether you know it or not. Whips and chains are not all what BDSM is about. It is about trust. As your lover, I will expect you to submit to me sexually. I don't mean like a slave, but I do want to look after you. I will reward you for this submission. That is important to me." He turned back round to face her, and she could see this was hurting him. "Do you want to leave?"

"Do you think I should?"

"*She* did."

"We have been thrown together by a very intense experience. We still have so much to learn about each other. What you have just said, I won't lie, scares me a little. Mainly because I don't know much about it. But right now, I am not going anywhere." She tentatively reached out and placed her hand over the front of his trousers, his cock instantly sprung to life. "James, you have given to me a lot recently. Will you let me give to you? I want to have you in my mouth."

"You don't have to."

"I want to."

He nodded his consent and she started to undo his belt buckle, then the zip of his jeans. She turned her attention to his cock, which was right in front of her face. It was perfect. He was broad and long; she would barely be able to fit more than half of him in her mouth. Slowly she licked up his length towards the tip and flicked her tongue over it. He let out a gravelly moan.

The next time Amy swirled her tongue all the way around his cock. She drew him into her mouth, shallowly at first, but as she moved up and down, she took him deeper and deeper, he was stretching her mouth. What would he feel like in her pussy? She cupped his balls, ran a finger over the tight skin underneath, and he grabbed hold of the unit next to them.

"Fuck, Amy."

Amy pulled back and took hold of her glass of Prosecco. She took some of the cooling bubbles into her mouth and then quickly took as much of his cock into her mouth as she could. He shuddered and hissed. She swallowed the wine.

"You are far too much of an expert at this. You sure you are a good girl?"

She gave a throaty laugh. Her pace quickened, and she was sucking him hard now, taking him deeper and deeper. She then withdrew to his tip leaving him bereft of the warmth of her mouth. She was tantalising the proud purple crown with little licks. This was all new to her but somehow she just knew how to please him.

"You will get the biggest reward ever for this sweetheart."

Amy knew he was getting close when she looked at where he gripped the unit. The whites of his knuckles were showing.

"Harder. Deeper."

She obeyed, and he hit the back of her throat. She gagged a little but swallowed him down.

"Amy, I am going to come. You don't have to take me, but I will need to pull out if you don't."

She allowed the word 'no' to reverberate around his cock and took him deep again. As she did, he came with ferocity; she could taste every pulsating wave of his essence. He withdrew from her mouth and Amy swallowed every last drop of him. James bent to kiss her, and he had the withdrawn expression of guilt on his face.

"Please tell me I didn't hurt you. That it wasn't too much. I am sorry. I got carried away."

Amy ran her hand over his cheek.

"No, James. It was perfect for me." She kissed him and nestled against his chest. His heartbeat was so fast. She couldn't tell whether it was because he had orgasmed or because he was terrified. "We will learn this together. Never shy from telling me anything, please."

He kissed the top of her head,

"I will try."

CHAPTER NINE

James

"We need to be certain on these figures. This deal has always been problematic, and I am not going to let it run away with us. Simon. What are your percentage errors allowance?" James stood at the head of the big board table, around him were his heads of departments, and they were discussing a contract for building properties in the South American market. James looked towards his head of Accounting; he was young for the position and an awful flirt, but he was reliable and had been consistently accurate in his calculations.

"I have allowed two percent fluctuation; this should be no more than one million pounds either way. I know it sounds a lot, but the market is borderline, and the specifications are tightly controlled. We have already greased the wheels, so we shouldn't have to deal with as much bureaucracy in the long term either. I would say the leeway is minus point-five to plus two point five percent. A lot of the work has been done upfront. To not sign now would give us a significant loss."

"And the plans?" James turned to his head of architecture.

"Agreed in principal, subject to your signature on the contract."

"Any repercussions; like over the tensions in the Falklands?" This time, it was his commercial director to whom he turned.

"Good publicity for improving them. Especially with your donations to the orphanage and women's refuge."

"So, if we put it to a vote?" Ultimately, any decision on the signing of contracts was his responsibility but he allowed his close team to convey their opinions to him. "A show of hands for yes?"

All of the team put their hands up.

"Motion carried. I will sign the documents tomorrow then"

At that moment, Matthew appeared. He made a sign that he needed to speak to him, and from the look on his face, it was something to do with Amy.

"Thank you everyone," James said.

Matthew walked in the door as the members of James' board left.

"What is it?"

"Miss Jones, Sir, she has boarded a train out to Essex."

"What?" James looked at him in astonishment.

"You didn't know."

"No, I didn't fucking know. Did she tell you? Why didn't you say anything before now? What the hell is she playing at?"

"She didn't tell me, Sir. I had a phone call from your mother, and she told me then. She assumed we knew and that Amy was with me."

"Does she have anyone with her?"

"Miss Anderson is tailing her, as requested. She won't interact unless vital for Miss Jones protection."

James pulled his phone out of his pocket and flicked onto a tracking app.

"What train is she on?"

"According to Miss Anderson, it is a fast train to Shenfield in Essex."

James rubbed at his temple before taking large steps from the room and back to his office. Marie stood to give him his messages as he passed, but he just waved her away. James went straight to his safe and pulled out the file. "Damn it. It is her mum's birthday today. Get the car. She must be going to her grave. She won't be thinking straight and she won't be looking out for danger. Why didn't she tell me? I could've taken her."

"Do you think that is wise?" Matthew didn't move. "Maybe she needs time alone for this. If Amy had wanted you there, she would have told you. She is safe. Miss Anderson is watching her, and she is good."

Matthew didn't often question James' orders that was one of the reasons that got on so well.

"I will be there for her afterwards. I won't impact on her mourning, but I am not risking anything happening to her. We still don't know what her uncle is up to. He was looking for something in that flat. We don't know if he found it or not. I have to protect her, Matthew. I won't lose her."

"James, she isn't Colette. She is completely different. You have to trust her."

James turned away and clenched his fists. "Don't even mention her name near me. Go get the car." The last words were spoken with cold demand. Matthew had pressed the wrong button. James was doing all he could to keep his mind when he was around Amy. He wanted to do so much to her, but it was wrong, all wrong. He needed to smother her and keep her safe, he needed to prove that he could put that part of his life aside and be the perfect boyfriend.

"As you wish, Boss."

When they pulled up outside the park that the app said Amy was in, Matthew turned to him again,

"Please let her have her moment alone, James. She lost both her parents so tragically, it will still be raw, especially after recent events."

"I will. Thank you, Matthew. I am sorry for my attitude earlier."

"I am used to it, Boss."

James got out of the car and wandered through the trees, past numerous statues of creatures he recognised from the story of the Gruffalo. He eventually saw Amy, sitting on a bench, talking to herself. She had tears in her eyes. A bunch of lilies lay by her feet. The steam of her breath flowed from her mouth as she spoke. James made no attempt to move forward. James could just about hear her voice; she was sobbing as she spoke. He wanted nothing more than to pull her into his arms and hold her, but he knew she needed space.

"I trusted him, mum, I thought he was all that I had left in the world, and he betrayed me in the worst way. Did you protect me from his real nature? You should have told me. Why didn't you say anything? You always treated me like a princess and hid the nastiness of the world from me. How am I supposed to protect myself now when I know nothing about real life?" James felt guilty, he was the one who had shown her what her uncle was.

Amy's one-sided conversation changed to a discussion on him. "I really like him, mum. He makes me feel so special. I know he is hiding so much from me, and I want to trust him, but I am scared. What if what he is hiding is dangerous? He is very intense, and everything feels so strange at the moment. I barely know what normal is anymore. Why did you have to die? I need you so much, I need to talk to you. Why did you leave me?" Her voice broke on the last words, and she collapsed her head down into her lap. James knew at that moment what it would do to him if he lost his mother, he saw it in Amy's breaking heart. He went to step forward to comfort her, but something stopped him. He couldn't give her that support just now as there was still had so much that he hadn't told her. James took a step back and turned back to the car. Matthew opened the door for him as he came alongside the vehicle.

"Take me to the nearest train station, Matthew. I will get a train back to London. I want you to return here and bring Amy home."

"You sure, boss?"

"Yes. She needs this time to herself. I don't say it often, but you were right."

"You are doing the right thing, James."

"I can't let it happen again, Matthew. I need to control this."

"No, you need to forget everything they did to you."

James looked up at his bodyguard as he sat.

"That will never happen."

"Why not?"

"Matthew, just drive."

"James, answer me this? What does she honestly know about you except that you have money?"

"Nothing."

"Then if you want to keep her, talk to her."

James looked out the window as Matthew turned the car around. Could he really take the risk and open up to her?

Amy

"Need a lift Miss Jones?"

Matthew pulled the Aston Martin Rapide S up to Amy.

"What are you doing here? How did you find me?"

"Tracked your phone." She should have known. "If you had told me where you were going, I would have brought you here as well. That is what I am here for. It is my job."

"I thought James may need you, and I didn't want to disturb you."

"I spend most of my time sitting around his office reading the newspaper."

"Sorry. I thought he kept you busy."

Amy wiped away the tears to try to disguise the fact that she had been crying but when he offered her a tissue she knew she had failed. They didn't really speak on the journey back to London. Amy was emotionally tired; she shut her eyes and must have fallen asleep for an hour as when she opened them they were pulling up outside James' house. She sat up and rubbed her sleepy eyes.

"Thank you, Matthew. I am sorry to have made you drive all that distance."

"Not a problem Miss, I like to get out of the city sometimes. Anytime you want to go to the country just ask. We'll take a picnic next time."

Amy laughed, but secretly vowed she would take him up on that offer. "Will you tell James what I did?" James was paranoid about her security, and in the few weeks she had been with him he always had ensured that either Matthew or himself accompanied her when she went out. She found it a little stifling after being able to travel where ever she wanted for the last few years but she also found a degree of comfort in it.

"If he asks, I will say I took you both ways."

"Thank you. I know he is worried about my uncle, but this was something I needed to do on my own."

"I know." He got out and came around to open the door for her before she could question him further. "Go on up. I better get going to pick up Mr North. Don't want him getting grumpy cause he has to get a tube with the regular people." Matthew's cheeky laugh made Amy chuckle as well. And a laugh was what she needed. "Miss Jones, can I just say something?"

"Of course."

"Don't give up on asking him about himself. He will open up eventually."

Miranda handed her a cup of tea as she entered the front door. "How was your day out?"

Amy pondered her answer. Miranda's question was so genuine and kindly put. The woman had been so helpful. She decided on the truth, even if it did get back to James. Matthew said he would cover for her on the aspects of her safety.

"I went back to Essex, where I grew up. There's a park there I visited lots with my mother. It was her birthday to-day, and I wanted to just sit and remember her for a few moments."

Miranda came up to her, put her arms around her, and brought Amy close, which took Amy a little by shock.

"That sounds a wonderfully comforting thing to do. The

small places always give us what we need in times of anguish. Come take a seat, you must be tired."

"I slept in the car on the way home."

"Have you told James that it was your mother's birthday?"

Amy shook her head, "I thought he would know. He has that file on me so I figured he would know everything already. He didn't say anything this morning, though."

"Oh Amy, dear. He is a man, he may have a file on you, but he has no idea how to use it. You will still have to remind him when your birthday is."

Amy felt deflated as she took a seat on the sofa. She really was naive in so many aspects. She knew nothing and was falling for a man of the world. He would probably tire of her soon and throw her back out on the street. Nobody could fall in love with someone that could barely tie their own shoe laces without some sort of advice.

"I will tell him later. Matthew has gone to collect him from work."

"I will leave you two alone tonight. You need some time together. Why don't you get a takeaway of your choice and just relax?"

"I would actually like to go out for dinner with him. It is not something we have done yet."

"Then tell him that. Amy, I know my son can be a little full on at times, I have no idea why, but his heart is kind. If you are not happy with something he wants to do, don't let him dictate to you."

"Do you stand up to him?" Amy bit her lip. She hadn't meant to ask the impertinent question, but it just seemed to roll off her tongue. Things often did. She really needed to learn to control that.

"It is alright Amy; I know that I am speaking of something that I don't often do myself. My son changed a few years ago. He wasn't always this closed off. He was attacked. I don't know the full details but I think it scared him. I am sure he will tell you about it, but he hasn't exactly been forthcoming with me. For now, though, you just need to know that, in all of this, you must keep to your strengths. That is what attracted him to you in the first place. You have a strong sense of your own wellbeing. If you want to go out to dinner, tell him. And make sure you choose the restaurant as well. I know that he seems to think he must do everything for appearances, but actually, he loves the simple things in life."

An idea suddenly hit Amy, she knew just what she was going to do and where she was going to take James for dinner. It was traditionally British but with an elegant flair. She got up from her seat and gave Miranda an immense hug. "I know exactly where I am going to take him. Matthew should be bringing him home soon, tell him I want him dressed in jeans and a t-shirt and ready to go by six-thirty." Amy set off back to her room as she spoke. "Oh and Miranda. He is to leave his wallet at home."

"I can't promise that last one, but I will tell him."

CHAPTER TEN

Amy

At just gone seven, Matthew pulled the car up outside a vintage fish and chip just by Liverpool Street Station. Amy was so excited she was almost bouncing in the car as they drove. James had a scowl on his face, Amy had heard him grumble at his mother when she had told him that he was to leave his wallet at home. As soon as she had appeared in her long jumper and leggings with knee high boots, James had quietened and reluctantly agreed. Miranda had given Amy a wink of good luck as they had left the building.

"What is this place?"

"It is a compromise."

"Compromise?"

"My treat for dinner. I would have taken you down to the coast for fish and chips, but that would be a long drive."

"We could've gone to the coast for dinner. That is what I have Matthew for. To drive us wherever we want to go." Matthew groaned at the front of the car. James got out of the car and held his hand out to help Amy from her seat.

"Matthew has already driven out that way today." Amy was going to tell him when they had gotten to the table, but the mood he was in, maybe outside in the open was easier.

"Why?" James didn't let go of her hand but lead her towards the restaurant.

"I went to where I grew up." Amy stopped just outside the entrance. "It would have been my mother's birthday today, we often went to a park together, and I wanted to go there to remember her." She bowed her head, this was crazy, she was feeling guilty for lying, "I...um...I got a train there." James' hand clenched tighter on hers.

"Alone?"

She nodded.

"I know."

Amy looked up and straight at James. His eyes were soft and full of affection for her. "You know? Matthew told you?"

"No, I saw you there."

"What?"

Amy let go of his hand and stepped back. He was there? He had been watching her?

"I don't understand."

"Matthew brought me down when I saw where you had gone. I thought you might need me when I realised it would have been your mum's birthday."

"But when Matthew found me, you weren't with him?"

"I got a train back to London."

"Why didn't you come to me?"

"Because you needed that time to yourself. It was a part of your grief and reflection on the last few weeks."

"It was."

James pulled her closer to him and brushed his hand through her hair.

"I know this is all still new, and we are getting to know each other, but you can talk to me about things like this. If you had mentioned it, I would have come with you but given you the time you needed to be alone." Amy kissed him lightly on the cheek. "So are we eating? I haven't had proper fish and chips for a long time now. I must have been a kid on Hasting's seafront the last time." James led Amy into the restaurant, and he allowed her to order for them. She had a glass of white wine, he had a beer, and they both had beer-battered fish with chips.

"Do you look like your mother?" James asked as he sampled the mushy peas.

"I do."

"Sophie is the spitting image of my mum as well. I think I have too much of my father in me."

"When was the last time you saw your dad?"

"I would rather not talk about him. He hurt my mother badly, and I need him out of my life forever."

"Alright. How about a favourite subject at school then?"

"What?"

"Come on, allow me some questions. You have a whole file on me of information, but I have to find out about you the old-fashioned way."

"History."

"History? I wouldn't have guessed that."

"Why?"

"I would have thought craft, design and technology."

"I like learning about people's pasts. How they lived."

"You are somewhat of an enigma. Shock me again?"

"With what?"

"Something else that I wouldn't expect from you?"

"There isn't really a lot to tell. What you see is what you get."

"I don't believe that for one minute. Come on? There must be something."

"Really, there isn't."

"Ok first kiss?"

"Colette, unfortunately. We were together when we were sixteen. Your kisses are so much better though."

"You lost your virginity to her?"

"No." Amy could see that he was getting reluctant to answer these questions, but she needed to know.

"Who then?"

"Amy, can we just enjoy this meal, please? Why don't you tell me your favourite subject at school instead?"

"English. Now answer my question."

"A prostitute."

"What?" Amy screeched her answer.

People turned to stare at them.

"I am not proud of it. It was just the one thing amongst my mates and me."

"Do you and your friends still use prostitutes?"

"They're no longer my buddies."

The look in James' eyes changed to one of shame, and she knew that she wouldn't get another answer from him on this subject.

"So you like history. Have you visited any of the old houses in the country?"

James looked straight into her eyes, the shame disappeared and was replaced by affection.

"Lots. I really want to take you to my place in Yorkshire. It is the stuff of Pride and Prejudice."

"I would like that very much."

"So, you said you were into this BDSM thing."

"Was. I am not any longer."

"Alright, but I read Fifty Shades of Grey. They seemed to enjoy it, well in parts. I don't think that woman. I forget her name...was interested in the contract part. Is that why Colette didn't want to do that?"

"Amy, we are having a nice meal. I really don't want to talk about my ex-girlfriend. She is out of my life, end of story." Somehow Amy didn't believe that one bit. Someone who was relaxed about ex relationships didn't change the subject every time they spoke about it.

"We are not talking about your ex-girlfriend. We are talking about BDSM. I want to know more about it."

"I don't do it anymore." James shoved a chip in his mouth and frowned at her.

"Humour me, alright?" Jesus, he could be so tetchy sometimes. She wished he would just tell her whatever it was that was buried so deep inside.

"You don't have to have contracts. It can be mutually agreed between two parties what you do. The Dom's job is to protect the sub, and in return she gives him her submission. Sometimes this is just sexually but in some couples it extends to him choosing what she eats, wears and more."

"So like the Dom would lay her clothes out for her in the morning?"

"Yes but he would reward her for that by washing her all over before she dresses."

"Would she have to wash him and get him dressed?"

"Depends on the nature of the agreement between them."

"Did you want this?"

"Partly."

"Partly?"

"I want to take care of any woman that is mine, and I am in a position to do so. I would want to buy her the best clothes to make her look and feel beautiful."

"That explains your insistence on our shopping trip."

"I wanted you to feel beautiful."

"I don't have body issues James, I have 'being beholden to someone' issues. My entire life has been governed. I want to be able to look after myself a bit."

"Even if it gets you into trouble?"

"You mean my uncle?"

"It was only a matter of time before he had an offer like I gave him, from someone that didn't have your best interests at heart."

"I know." Amy looked down and shuffled a bit of fish across her plate. "So BDSM basically means the woman putting her day to day control into the hands of a man?"

"Only if both parties agree."

"Hmm. And what about the sex stuff? Is that why you won't let me come until you say I can? Or is that just you being bossy?"

"You are impatient. Too much playing with yourself, if you ask me."

"Hey. I don't. Well I do...but we are not talking about that." Amy couldn't believe that part of the conversation had come up.

"Of course. Was the orgasm I gave you good?"

"Yes."

"Better than when you do it yourself?"

"Yes," she thought about it for a second and then added, "but I thought you weren't a Dom anymore?"

"Part of it will never leave me. But the scenes and stuff I

will never do again. It is wrong."

"Scenes?"

"Yes. There are certain clubs that you can go to and perform more exotic acts with women. You can also perform
these in a private bedroom as well."

"You mean like my uncle's clubs," Amy rolled her eyes.

"No, clubs where both are willing participants, and they
consensually agree to engage in acts, without money changing hands."

"Oh. You use these clubs often?"

"Not anymore."

"You have spanked me a couple of times when we have
been playing. Is that part of it? Because I don't remember
my ex-boyfriend doing that."

"Don't mention your ex-boyfriend. I don't wish to know
he existed."

"And the spanking?" Amy was on a roll. She wasn't going
to let up on her questioning.

"I shouldn't do that. I will stop."

"Why?"

"I shouldn't do it."

"What if I liked it?"

"You don't."

"How do you know?"

"I just do."

He was shutting down again. She was going to get nowhere with that question. Even if she did like the spanking.

"Is your fish good?"

"Yes. I will probably need to do double my gym session
tomorrow but I am enjoying it."

"Good." Amy was trying her hardest to think of more
questions to get him to open up again. She knew she would
probably have to do most of her research on the internet.
"How long have you had the tattoo? I want a tattoo. I don't
know what yet, though."

"A few years now. If you decide you want one, I will
take you to my artist. He is the best. You don't go anywhere

else."

"I don't go anywhere else?"

"Yes."

"Is that a Dom thing?"

"No it is an *I have the best artist* thing."

"Why the angel?"

"I liked the design."

"Did it hurt?"

"A lot."

"How long did it take?"

"Three sittings. How is your book coming? Have you had any more time to write it?"

And that was the end of that. He had shut her down again. Still, she had gotten more out of him than previously. Amy was determined, she wasn't going to stop.

They finished the rest of the meal. When it came to the bill, Amy snatched it before he could pay and went straight to the cashier. She felt smug until, the next morning, she found the money had been transferred to her bank account. He may deny he was into BDSM, but Amy had a feeling that he was more into it than he realised.

CHAPTER ELEVEN

James

James could not believe that Amy hadn't walked out on him.

When he'd told Colette what he wanted sexually, she'd laughed at him and ended their relationship. She had insulted him, and he had had to buy Colette off to prevent her from selling stories about him. He had forked out a good million. It had nearly broken him. Thankfully they had signed contracts and she could not come at him for any more money when his business didn't falter but prospered.

James longed to try new things with Amy. She was under his skin and in his head. She tested his control but took him entirely when he demanded it.

James shook his head. He was at his desk in the middle of his London office, and he was fantasising about her. James hadn't invited Amy to his office. He had wanted to protect her from any scrutiny at the hands of prying employees—well mainly his secretary—but he picked up the phone and pressed the quick dial for home.

"Hi, James. You alright?"

"Are you dressed?"

"I have a towel around me. I can dress in a few minutes. Why?"

"Just a towel? You want to send me a picture...without the towel."

"Mr North, I hope your work calls are not monitored."

"Miss Jones, I am the chairman of the company. I will have them erased."

She giggled playfully. His cock jumped.

"Hush and listen." She instantly hushed. "I want you to bring my lunch to the office. Bring some for yourself. I don't have many meetings today. I want to show you around." She was silent, had he said something wrong? "Amy?"

"What should I wear?"

"What you usually wear." He chuckled as he answered. "Jeans, jumper, boots."

"You sure? I have a smart skirt and jacket I can wear."

"Amy, come as you."

"Are you sure?"

"Yes. Don't forget my favourite pickle."

"That stuff makes your breath stink."

"You planning on kissing me in public?"

"Not if you eat the pickle."

"Amy."

"I will be there in half an hour."

She put the phone down. James pulled up his instant messenger and quickly typed.

Actually, wear the skirt...no knickers.
J

She replied instantly with a picture of her middle finger. He laughed.

Amy arrived pretty much on the half hour. Matthew escorted her up, and when his secretary tried to stop them, Matthew just scowled at her and said that Amy was Mr North's girlfriend. His secretary's face was a picture. James suppressed a chuckle and stood to greet them.

"Marie, it is fine. I asked Matthew to bring Amy up. Amy this is my secretary Marie. Marie, my girlfriend, Amy. Marie gave the best-nonplussed greeting she could muster and Amy reciprocated with all her sweetness. James nodded to Matthew,

"Thank you. I will call you when Miss Jones is ready to leave." His bodyguard left. "Amy, this way?" He placed his hand on the small of her back and guided her into his office, shut the door behind them and flicked a switch to turn the glass opaque.

"She fancies you."

"I hadn't guessed." He chuckled.

"That was mean. You should have told her I was coming before I appeared."

"She will live. She has read far too many romantic books where the millionaire boss falls for his secretary. She wants a fantasy; the reality is very different." She raised her eyebrow at him and he motioned for her to lay out his lunch.

"You shouldn't lead her on."

"Are you jealous?"

"No."

"She is excellent at her job, and part of that is probably because she wants to please me. What is the harm in that?"

"Just watch that she doesn't send you to all the wrong meetings tomorrow."

They both laughed.

"Did you follow my instructions?"

Amy opened her bag and laid out sandwiches and a salad on the table.

"What?"

"You are wearing a skirt, but what is underneath?"

She sighed heavily and slid her hands down the silky fabric of her skirt. She gripped the end of it and pulled slowly up to reveal her slender, toned thigh. Amy rolled it even further, watching him the entire time, awaiting his reaction but he gave nothing away. Finally, she pulled the skirt all the way up and revealed to him that she was indeed not wearing any underwear. He ran his tongue over the back of his teeth as he savoured her neatly trimmed pussy.

"Satisfied?"

"Not yet. Touch yourself, Amy."

"Not here."

He switched on the authority in his tone.

"Touch yourself, Amy."

Her hand went between her thighs. James watched as

she slid a perfectly manicured finger over the folds of her sex.

"What would you like me to do now?"

"I want you to make yourself come."

"Do you have security cameras in your office?"

"Of course I do."

"Monitored?" She moved her hand away from herself.

He reached out and pressed a button on the phone. It rang twice before it was answered.

"Mr North? How can I help?"

"I want all the cameras switched off in my office immediately."

"Sir?"

"Please, Harry."

"At once, sir." There was a small background noise. "All done, sir."

'Thank you. Turn them all back on in an hour." He hung up. "Happy?" He smiled at Amy.

"Has anyone ever said no to you?"

"Doesn't happen often."

"I will have to remember that."

"Enough talking Amy."

"Bossy."

He slid his hands down to his hardened cock. He undid the zip, pulled himself out, and began stroking his cock. Amy put her hand down and circled her clit. She held herself so that he could see everything. She was breathing heavily, and her perfect breasts swelled within her t-shirt. James wanted to touch her, but he wanted to watch her satisfy herself, first. He gripped himself harder, his control was wavering. Amy was getting close; he knew the soft whimpering noise she made already. She was breathing harder and harder and her head fell back against the edge of the chair.

"Don't come yet Amy."

"Fuck you."

When her eyes flashed open, she met his gaze with intense ferocity. James lost his control. He rushed forward, grabbed her hands, and held them above her head. His weight pressed against her, his cock close to the entrance of her sex. All he needed to do was push inside her.

James' face was inches from hers, and her eyes glistened with devilment. She was testing him.

"I should deny you for that."

"You won't."

"Do you really want to test me?"

James took both of her hands in one of his and the other went to his cock. He thrust hard into his hand and came instantly upon her thigh. He groaned out loud as his soul poured out of him and marked her delicate flesh as his. He could scarcely believe this was happening, she looked beautiful with his cum on her. She was definitely his now, not that she hadn't been from the first moment that he had seen her. James looked up, and she was watching everything. He let go of her hands and put himself back in his trousers.

"Keep your hands above your head." She did as he asked, and he went to his sink, got a cloth, brought it back to her, and cleaned her thigh. "Right, I need to show you the office. Up you get."

"James?" her eyes were full of questioning.

"Punishment, Amy. You wanted to test my limits."

She sat up and pulled her skirt down.

"Really?"

"Really." James smirked.

Amy huffed, but she stood and took his hand.

The tour of the office seemed to take a long time.

Everyone had heard the boss had a girlfriend from Marie, and they all wanted to meet her and talk with her. Amy was polite and took her time to speak to everyone, but she had a healthy glow to her cheeks. She was seething at him for this punishment. If he hadn't had just come, he would be hard again with the excitement of watching her. After about an hour and a half, they finally finished and James saw Amy into the lift back down to the car park. He got in with her, and as the lift started descending he pulled her to him. She had waited long enough. Before she could argue he had his hand under her skirt and massaging her clit.

"Are you going to be a good girl this time, Amy?" He removed his pressure.

"James, please." James could tell she no longer cared they were in a lift and it could stop at any time and someone else get in. All she wanted was to orgasm at his touch. It was all he wanted now as well. He gave her what she needed again, harder, circling the little nub in tantalising pleasure.

"Come, Amy. Come, now."

She did, shuddering and pulsating against him, her groans of euphoria causing him to hiss into her neck in need. He was rock hard again and longed to just sink balls deep into her but he had made a promise. He would keep it even if it killed him. James held her tight as he felt her legs caving. The lift stopped.

James righted her skirt and almost carried her to the car. He knew she couldn't speak, so quietly he placed her in the Aston Martin to a questioning look from Matthew.

"I think all the questioning was a bit much. Miss Jones is fatigued."

Matthew nodded.

"I will see her home safely, Sir."

"Thank you, Matthew."

James watched the car pull away and brought his hand to his nose. The smell of Amy's orgasm was on it. The guilt suddenly washed over him. What had he done?

CHAPTER TWELVE

Amy

Amy could feel the throb of that orgasm between her thighs for days. She was floating. He had denied her, she had struggled not to touch herself for almost two hours, and then he'd touched her and she exploded. It had been in a lift. Damn. What if it had CCTV? James would get rid of any evidence, she was sure. She wondered if he could get the tape for them to watch together. Amy shook the thought from her head.

Where was Matthew? He was late.

Amy hadn't told James, but she had made a decision. They were testing each other's limits. James had been close to pushing inside her, and he would have come the second he did.

It was too risky.

Amy had booked the appointment to get checked and make sure she was clean. After Amy had discovered about James and his ex-girlfriend and the prostitute he had left a file for her detailing that he had regular annual checks and that the last one was shortly after Lanzarote. Amy was his girlfriend now, and as such, she needed to take precautions to prevent any unwanted accidents.

Matthew finally buzzed up, and she grabbed her Mulberry handbag and raced down to the car.

"I need to go to Kennington Lane please, Matthew."

"Of course, Miss." He drove away and Amy checked her watch. She had twenty minutes until her appointment. Hopefully, the traffic was going to be good. She looked out the window as the sights of London sped past. As they rounded Green Park, they headed north.

"Matthew, this isn't the way."

"It is, Miss."

Her phone rang before she could answer him.

"James, is it urgent? Matthew has taken the wrong direction."

"No, he hasn't. He is taking you to my private physician at Harley Street. "I am sorry, Amy. If I had known earlier what you were planning, we could've discussed it together and I could've come with you. This is something we are both in together."

"What?" Amy couldn't believe what he was saying. "How did you know?"

"Amy, I told you, I know everything about you."

Amy didn't know whether to be flattered he cared so much or annoyed that he had told her what to do again and was paying for it. "There is nothing wrong with my doctor. Matthew will be there the entire time. Well not in the examining room but...oh you know what I mean. I will be safe."

"I mean no offence to your doctor, but mine is the best money can buy. He will offer you the best advice and give you the right contraception for our needs."

He had smooth-talked her around. "Ask me before you change my plans next time. That is all I ask."

"You can punish me later." She could hear him chuckling.

"Go do some work Mr North, I have to go spread my legs for your doctor."

Amy laughed.

"Do whatever he suggests. Don't think of the cost. Phone me when you are done."

"I will. Later."

"Goodbye."

Amy hung up.

"Is everything alright with the change of plans Miss Jones?" Matthew looked at her through the mirror. He looked guilty.

"Matthew, do you tell James wherever I ask you to take

me?"

"It is what he pays me to do Miss."

"He is as bossy with you, then."

"Always." He laughed.

"Matthew, one thing he can't make you do, though, is call me Miss Jones. I give you permission to call me Amy. Please do so."

"As you wish Miss....Amy." He stopped the car, "We are here." He got out of the car and came to open the door for her, "Just up those steps."

Amy had never been to Harley Street. There were so many doctor's practices. She chuckled and thought maybe she should enquire about getting her beasts enlarged while she was here. See if that got back to James. He would have a fit. She went to reception, told them her name, and she was escorted into a private room and offered a drink from a vast menu of branded beverages. She decided on just water but even then had to choose a particular make, though she'd expected it to just be from the tap. The doctor appeared almost immediately after her drink had been brought. Amy was suddenly very nervous; this all felt really serious. She didn't need to worry, though, Doctor Baudin was very friendly. She examined Amy and gave her a clean bill of health, a blood test was taken, and she promised the results would be available later that day and couriered straight to her. They discussed various forms of contraception, many Amy didn't even know existed. Amy was given the injection but was told to be careful for seven days as she wouldn't be covered until then.

James was going to India in two days. She wouldn't see him for at least a week. Amy thanked the doctor and was told the bill had been sorted by Mr North. Amy didn't argue. She probably couldn't afford the prices in here anyway.

It was the start of April and exceptionally warm. Amy had been cooped up in the house for a long time, so she asked Matthew to drop her at the North side of Kensington Gardens on the way back, and she would walk home from there. He grumbled his reluctance, but she insisted and he had no choice but to obey her. The gardens were full of spring colour. Tulips and daffodils lined the walkways. Amy looked to the sky, shut her eyes, and inhaled deeply. She was in the middle of a very busy city but it was so peaceful here. She had to get James to walk here with her. Maybe she could ask him to take the day off before he went to India. Spend the whole day just the two of them together.

As Amy rounded the corner of the Serpentine by the Princess Diana memorial, her peace was shattered when she was suddenly set upon by a man with a camera and a woman holding an iPhone to her mouth.

"Miss Jones, tell me what is it like to be dating one of the most eligible billionaires in the UK? Where did you meet him? Is he as good in bed as the rumours say? Can we get a picture of you posing by the fountain?"

The camera flashed in her eyes and she blinked. "Who are you?"

"Sally Bridgewater, London Daily Magazine. Come on Miss Jones, no need to be so shy. Mr North is quite the catch. You are a very lucky girl."

The camera flashed again and people stopped to stare. Amy felt very exposed.

"I don't wish to talk about my relationship. If you would excuse me." She went to push past the buzzing paparazzi but Sally Bridgewater was persistent.

"Come on, just one quote for our readers. Is he as sexy under those suits as we all imagine?"

Amy was suddenly hoisted backwards. A lady she had never seen before stepped in front of her.

"Miss Jones has no comment. If you have any questions, you will address them to Mr North's press secretary, as is proper. Miss Jones, this way, please. Matthew is waiting in the car to escort you home."

The lady grabbed her arm and pulled her away from the now-sullen Miss Bridgewater. Amy tugged her arm free.

"Who are you?"

"Sonia, Miss Jones, I am your personal security."

"My what?"

"Miss Jones, the car, please. We need to get you away."

"No." Amy turned and began to walk off in the other direction from where she was being led. Her phone rang, and she didn't need to look at it to know who was ringing. She knew. "When were you going to tell me you were having me followed everywhere?"

"Please go with Sonia."

"No."

"Amy."

"Fuck you, James."

She hung up. The phone rang again, but she didn't answer. She muted it and put it back in her bag. Amy hurried out of the park, though she didn't really know where she was going. Sonia was probably following her.

He was supposed to not keep secrets from her, yet he had someone following her around. Why hadn't he just introduced her to Sonia? She understood the need for protection. Without thinking, she slammed her fist into a nearby wall. People around her began to stare.

"What are you looking at?" She shouted at the onlookers.

Matthew pulled up in the car beside her. "Amy get in, please."

She folded her arms across her chest and refused to budge.

"Please, Amy. If I don't get you back to the house safely, it will be more than my life is worth. I know him. He will have left the office and be heading home now. He is scared you will get hurt. That is the only reason he did this."

Amy rolled her eyes and sighed with defeat. She opened the door and got in the car. Sonia jumped in the front seat next to Matthew. The short journey to the house was made in silence. When they arrived, Amy didn't wait to have the door opened for her but stormed into her new home without so much as a thank you. She was so angry, she was fuming. Her knuckle hurt and was bleeding but most of all had realised that the freedom she had had in the past was gone. Did she want this?

She felt enclosed, claustrophobic.

Amy went to the kitchen sink and took a cloth and washed her knuckles. She heard the front door open and James called out her name. He was angry.

"In the kitchen." She kept her back to the door and washed her hand. James thundered into the room and threw his briefcase on the counter.

"What did you think you were doing? You never not answer the phone to me, Amy. Look at me." His voice was full of fury but had undercurrents of deep concern. Amy turned. Tears had started to tumble down her pale cheeks. The cloth she held at her hand was covered in watery blood. "Jesus." James halted in shock. "What happened? Did they do this? I will sue every last penny out of them." He rushed forward and grabbed her hand and checked it. He brought it to his lips to kiss it but Amy pulled her hand away.

"I did it. You lied to me, James. I asked you not to and you did it again. In fact, you did it all morning. You cancelled my appointment and rearranged it with your Doctor. I know you have a need to control but...." She stopped and turned away again.

James stumbled backwards and took hold of the counter. "You want to leave me?"

Amy couldn't turn to face him just yet. She needed to figure this out without looking at him. "I know you need to control and I accept that. In many ways I like it. You look after me and ensure I am safe when I can't do it myself, but you need to tell me what you are doing." She took a deep breath and turn back to face him. He looked so scared. Neither had spoken of the feelings that were developing between them but they were starting to run deep on both sides. "If you had told me about Sonia, I might have complained for a few hours, but I know the reasons you are doing it. James, I know that in your business you just do things and people follow suit but this is not a business, this is a relationship. We are in it together. No more secrets from me. Please, James."

"'You are not leaving me." He took a tentative step towards her.

"If you promise me here and now that important matters such as personal protection or things which cost large sums of money will be discussed between us as adults, then I will stay."

Amy expected him to come and cradle her in his arms but he didn't. He reached for his briefcase. "I should tell you about this then?"

Amy was instantly worried. What now?

"Our relationship has hit the gossip press and I have arranged an interview tomorrow for us both to officially come out as a couple."

"Alright. It isn't with that foul woman from the Park?"

"No someone much nicer."

"Good, anything else?"

"Will you to accompany me to India. I want you to be at my side throughout the entire opening. I want everyone to know that you are my girlfriend. Please, Amy. I have sorted a visa for you and everything."

"India?"

"Yes. I may want to surprise you, and keep that a secret, but you have my word. Big decisions I will talk to you about. What do you say, Amy, will you come with me? Be my partner for all the world to see?"

She smiled. "You better take me shopping for summer clothes."

CHAPTER THIRTEEN

James

James rolled over in the bed and his arm felt Amy's smooth, naked frame in the bed next to him. It wasn't a dream. They hadn't slept together before, but last night it just seemed the right thing to do. They hadn't been intimate in any way. It was not the time for that. They had just laid on the bed in each other's arms until they had fallen asleep. He had totally lost it yesterday when he got the phone call from Matthew saying that Amy was being hounded by Sally Bridgewater. His lawyers were now working on an injunction against her. When Amy had refused to answer the phone to him, however, he had almost combusted. She defied him but mostly he was scared. He was afraid that he had pushed her too far and that she would walk away from him. James had never felt this way about anyone before. She was driving him crazy. He wrapped his arms around her as she stirred, her bright blue eyes opened and greeted him.

"Morning, beautiful." He kissed her lips.

"Morning, handsome. You sleep well?"

"Best sleep I have ever had."

Amy nuzzled closer into him.

"What time are the magazine people coming?"

"Around ten. They will bring someone to do your hair and makeup. They will have someone find the perfect clothes for you as well. I have to do a phone call with India at nine, but I am not going to the office today."

"That is good. As long as they dress me in clothes I like." She looked at the clock. "So we have half an hour more in bed."

"Well, I was going to make you a cup of tea and breakfast in bed?"

"Oh. That gives me a big dilemma. I would like breakfast in bed but I also want to lay in your arms a bit longer."

"Decisions, decisions." James ran a hand down her stomach.

"Breakfast, please."

He groaned. "Really?"

"Go."

He slid from the bed and pulled on a pair of jogging bottoms. He could feel Amy's heated gaze scan over his body as he did.

"My wish is your command, Miss Jones. But just so you know, in future, I have an intercom into the kitchen and could've asked mum to bring it and leave it outside the door instead." Before Amy could say anything, he pulled his T-shirt over his head and left her moaning.

His mother was in the kitchen preparing breakfast as normal. He kissed her cheek.

"How is Amy this morning?"

"Nervous."

"You sure about this, James? You are not pushing her too quickly are you? You have only been together for just over a month."

"If I could hide her away and protect her from all of this I would, mum. I am terrified of losing her."

"You need to tell her everything, James."

"I know. I am going to book a week off after the opening in India. Maybe go to the Seychelles or Maldives. I will tell her everything then." He shrugged. "But for now, I need to get her breakfast."

His mum handed him a tray full of pastries and coffee.

"One step ahead of you."

"Thanks, mum."

"I will make myself scarce today."

"You don't have to."

"Oh I do, I have a date."

James' mouth dropped in shock.

"You have a what?"

"Take Amy her food or she will get hungry."

"Mum..."

"Go, James. I will be careful."

He shuddered. "Mum, I don't need to know that."

"I meant I would follow all your security advice."

"Phew." He picked up the tray and wandered back into the bedroom. Amy had gotten out of bed and wrapped a dressing gown around her naked body. James felt deflated, he had hoped to have some fun with Amy. A quick glance at the clock showed him there wouldn't be time anyway. If he were late for his call, there would be trouble.

"Here, beautiful. Breakfast." She turned, took the tray from him, and gave him a peck on the cheek.

"I will take it back to your mum and eat there. You get ready for your call." She kissed him again and smiled, "We can breakfast in bed tomorrow." And with a cheeky wink she meandered off back down the hallway. James ran a hand through his hair and sighed. God, he hoped she was ready to have sex soon. His balls were tight and turning blue, and he felt like he was permanently stiff when she was around. It was time for a shower. A freezing cold one. Again.

James could barely concentrate on his phone call. They had important final details to confirm, but all he could think about was Amy and this damn interview. Why couldn't they leave her alone? So what if he had a girlfriend? He wasn't a famous rock star, actor, or royalty, why couldn't they go and pester one of them instead? He never realised that by being a supposedly good looking billionaire meant you had no private life. He guessed it was his own fault because he was also seen out with different girls at different celebrity functions. He had a reputation as a play boy, the truth couldn't have been much further from what the press saw. He would have been quite happy to have not attended them, but he didn't have a choice. It was what was required to keep the business in the spotlight.

When they finished, he went to find Amy. The stylists and the reporter were already there, and Amy was in the centre of a hive of activity. She had someone curling her hair in soft waves that accentuated the perfect features of her face. They were using a scary looking piece of equipment though and James hoped it wouldn't leave any permanent damage. Amy smiled at him and held her hand out. He took it and pressed a kiss to the soft skin. A camera flashed, and he turned and glared.

"Mr North." The reporter stood and held his hand out to him. James shook it. The journalist was a little too enthusiastic and made James feel a little uneasy, especially when he looked down at James's crotch with a lick of his lips. "It is so good to meet you, finally. I am sorry, Ellie couldn't make it so she sent me instead. I am Sean. Your girlfriend is just so lovely. A perfect little doll." He turned to her and winked. "We are making her look very natural." He turned back and looked James up and down again. "I think you need to complement her. I would say a nice pair of tight jeans and a plain T-shirt. That will be perfect."

"I wear what I want to," James replied in a sullied voice.

"Oh no, James. You have to wear what you are told. Besides, I like the idea of tight jeans." He raised a questioning eyebrow at her. Sean enthusiastically bounced next to him.

"Let us go and check out your wardrobe, Mr North. I am sure you have something suitable." Before James could have a chance to protest he was swept up by the reporter and led to his room. He could hear Amy laugh as he went. She would suffer for that later. Only he knew she wouldn't. He didn't do that anymore. He couldn't.

The interview started off well, general questions on how they met, how long they had been dating, that sort of thing. Amy held her own with the questions. She even admitted to being a dancer when questioned on what her job was. James was proud of her. However, when the sexual questions started, James was on the verge of kicking the reporter out of his house

"So Miss Jones, we have all seen pictures of Mr North after he has been exercising and has his shirt off. He is very toned. I know a lot of our female readers would like to lick his abs and see where else he is particularly toned." Sean paused and looked James over again. Why did they have to send me the gay interviewer who has spent most of the interview trying to come onto me? Did they think that would make him want to do more work with their magazine? Amy squeezed his hand in reassurance. "Are you able to give our readers an insight into what lies beneath all those fabulous designer suits and how talented he is with it?"

James went to hold his hand up to stop the interview but Amy took hold of it and smiled.

"Well, I am not sure if that is something we can talk about in public, because it is a very private thing between us. But I know you have loyal readers, so all I will say is..."

James held his breath. What was she going to say? And how much would he have to pay his lawyers to get that taken out of the interview?

"He is even better in the flesh than the pictures, and as for his talent? I can completely assure all your readers here and now; I am not with him for his money." She giggled and licked her lips; it sent shivers down his spine. He wanted to pin her to the sofa and fuck her while still doing the interview.

"Hmm. I can see. You are a very lucky lady indeed." Sean licked his lips.

James jumped to his feet, realised that gave a better view to Sean of his now even more snugly fitting jeans and quickly jumped behind a chair.

"The interview is done. I have work I need to do. I trust you got everything you need?"

"I certainly did." Sean got to his feet. He held out his hand, "It has been a pleasure, Mr North. A great pleasure indeed."

James reluctantly shook his hand again and quickly headed for the door.

"Amy can you see them out, please? I need to make a phone call."

Amy nodded and James returned to his office as quick as possible. He pulled up his laptop and checked his email. Nothing of any importance. He would still answer a few, though just so he could stay in his office.

Just as he finished, Amy entered the room.

"It is safe to come out now."

"Don't." He looked up at her and glared.

"Oh come on, it wasn't that bad. I was terrified but he put me at ease."

"Well, he didn't do that to me."

She came over to him and put her arms around his shoulders.

"My poor baby. Did the nasty man mentally undress you?"

"Amy."

She laughed again.

He should think of a reason to leave the house until he could calm down.

"I am sorry." She leaned forward and kissed his cheek. The heat of her lips pulsated through his body straight to his cock. Fuck, he really had to get out of there.

"I have to go to the office. Some forms need signing before I go to India." He stood up and went to the window to put distance between them both. He was shaking, his fists clenched to try to maintain control.

"Can you not have Matthew bring them over here? I thought we could have some lunch together and then maybe go for a walk."

"Matthew is not here to courier papers around for me, Amy. He is here for protection. If I were to have a walk with you, he would need to be with us." He snapped at her.

"I am sorry." He could hear the pain in her voice. This was killing him. "I will go change. I will see you tonight."

"Amy." She paused, her head was down. "I am sorry. That guy threw me off. I wanted to enjoy the interview. I

wanted it to be the first of many we do together. You did
well. I am proud of you."

She turned back to face him.

"Now you know how I feel when you look at me that
way."

He came up to her and dared to put his arms around her
waist, but he waited to be thumped and pushed away.

"You don't like the way I look at you?"

"I didn't say that."

"I am sorry I shouted at you."

"I know. I am sorry I teased you."

James was relaxing again. He was bringing himself back
under control. Just her closeness tamed the wild beast within him. He kissed her tenderly on the lips.

"Do you really have to go to the office."

He shook his head. "No."

"We can have lunch together?"

"Yes."

"Can we have lunch in bed?"

"Of course."

She took his hand and led him from the study. Instead of
heading to the kitchen she went straight to the bedroom,
though.

"Amy we need to get the food first."

She looked at him from under her long flutter lashes,

"I was thinking of a different type of lunch."

James stopped dead. Did she mean what he thought she
meant?

"James, I want you. In every way, a boyfriend and girlfriend should be together."

"Are you sure?"

"I trust you. In fact, I think I maybe falling in love with
you."

He couldn't speak. He had known from the moment he
first saw her in Lanzarote he was in love with her. Could he
do this? Should he do this?

She didn't know the truth of his past.

No, that was just what it was. It was his past.

Amy was his future, and she was standing there in front of him offering everything that he wanted. He growled,

"Get in the bedroom Amy, because I am not going to let you change your mind. I am going to make love to you until you can no longer walk."

Amy & James

Amy took James' hand and held it tight. He pulled her towards him, and a passionate kiss engulfed them both. She parted her lips slightly, and he delved his tongue inside her mouth to taste her sweetness. She could feel the urgency of the heat building inside her already. She had never wanted a man as much as she wanted James right now. She needed him tasting her body, she needed him inside her. She ached for it.

They were still in the hallway, though. Amy had enjoyed their first time up against a wall together, but she wanted more time to explore. She pulled her mouth away, breathless, and relished the taste of him on her lips.

"James, I want to take this slowly. I want to learn your body. Can we go to the bedroom please?"

He sighed, scooped her into his strong arms, kicked his bedroom door open, placed her tenderly on the bed, and went back to shut the door.

"My hero." She laughed and pulled her top over her head to reveal her breasts in a lacy cream bra. She pushed them together a little with a smirk.

James quickly flipped her over and brought her back against his taut body. Amy could feel the strain of his cock within his trousers.

Amy turned in his arms. He was standing at the end of the bed, and she was on her knees in front of him. The air was thick with the sexual anticipation between them, as she slowly started to unbutton his shirt. Neither said anything, they just watched as her delicate fingers lingered over each of the buttons in a tantalising reveal of his broad chest. She gasped as she dropped his shirt over his shoulders. He had the most beautiful body she had ever seen. It was hers to learn to pleasure in ways he liked. And learn everything she would. She reached her hand out to trail a path over one of his pecs and up his shoulder to where the feathers of his tattoo started. It was intricately designed. As she placed her finger at the start, he hissed and abruptly grabbed her hand.

"No."

Amy looked at him hesitantly. Why would he not want her to touch it? She leaned forward and kissed his lips again.

"It is an amazing design. Let me look at it please?"

He again shook his head, his eyes still carnally focused but Amy saw the sadness buried deep behind them. What did this tattoo mean? He was not telling her something again. Why did he have to do this? She wanted to know everything about him. She'd accept this little secret for now.

James reached around her body to unfasten her bra. He slowly and softly circled a finger around her left breast to where its peak stood proudly erect. He leant forward, taking it between his teeth and holding it while his tongue moistened the bud. Amy let her head fall back and groaned. This man did wonders with his tongue. She could think of so many more things she wanted him to explore with it. Tentatively, Amy reached for the waistband of his trousers. She needed to see him fully naked. His cock was beautiful. She knew what it felt like to have it within her, and she wanted that again. James, however, had other ideas, and he pushed her back against the bed. He trailed a path down her body, taking in every element of her taste and storing it for exploration further at a later date. He reached the waist band of her jeans and undid the zip. She was wet and her very core was throbbing. This teasing between them was killing her. She wanted him to touch her where she needed him the most. He looked up, grinned, and then helped her to shimmy the jeans over her slender legs.

"James please."

"Patience Amy. I am going to make this special for you,

for both of us."

She thrust her hips into the path of his hands. He slapped at her thigh.

"I am seriously going to have to punish you one day."

Amy giggled but stopped as soon as she saw a flash of pain flicker behind James' eyes again. She reached up and brought his lips down to hers. They kissed again, their eyes open, captured by the overwhelming emotions bonding them together. James broke the moment by tearing her pants from her body. He was beginning to make a habit of that. At least she now had what seemed like an endless supply of them after she had returned home one day to find her wardrobe looked like a lingerie shop.

Amy was naked before him. With her ex-boyfriend, she had always felt a little self-conscious in this position, but with James she knew that he adored her body and how much he craved every part of her. She lowered her eyes to see the straining need, which he still insisted being kept encased within his trousers.

James left a path of kisses over her body as he lowered to between her thighs, kissing either side of where she needed to be touched. She thrust her hips forward again, and he bit lightly the skin of her left thigh, sending shivers through her body. Her core ignited and she felt she may come just from that one touch. God this man played her like no other. He knew how to control her so that her body responded to everything that he did.

In the back of his throat, James gave a gravelly groan. It reverberated around Amy as he finally parted her wet folds and traversed his tongue up them.

"You taste perfect Amy" he said looking into her eyes, "I have never experienced anything like it before. You are what I have always dreamed off."

He bent again and dipped his tongue within her sweet haven. Amy cried out as he rubbed a finger over her straining clit. She was ready to explode. She needed to come, but stopped herself. She wanted James's consent. As he delved his tongue deeper and kept up the pressure on her engorged bud, she writhed on the bed.

"James, please. I need to come. Oh. Please."

He removed his tongue, mid thrust, and she moaned at the loss.

"Come, Amy, Come."

His tongue thrust straight back into her with a finger as well and she exploded. He held her tight until she stopped shuddering and then stood up beside her and freed himself from his jeans.

"I could watch you come all day Amy. It is the most amazing sight. You ready for some more?"

"More?" She was breathless and could barely feel her legs as it was. "More."

He chuckled, "Oh yes. Much more."

James reached in a drawer and pulled out a condom packet. Amy watched as he tore it with his teeth and then rolled the rubber barrier over his throbbing length. His magnificent cock was going to tear her apart. He seemed bigger than in Lanzarote. If that was possible. He was thick and long and his purple head oozed pre-cum into the condom.

Their mouths met again as James slid up her body, skin on skin, her legs parted wide, and as James positioned himself at her entrance, Amy looked down. He was about to slide into her. She tensed a little as his cock breached her and slowly slid in, inch by inch. He paused when he was about halfway. Allowing her to adjust to the feel of him. She was stretched wide but the tinge of pain brought her pleasure.

"Are you alright?"

Amy looked up from where she and James were joined and met the concerned hues of her lover's eyes. She exhaled a long breath that she didn't even realise had been held.

"I can feel you gripping tight on me, is it hurting?"

Amy gave him a reassuring smile and kissed him.

"I am fine; I am watching us." Her eyes flicked down again to where James' cock was half in her. James' eyes followed hers.

"Fuck." He hissed and pressed another inch in.

"You are so big, James but my body already doesn't want you to leave."

He gently thrust the last few inches in and filled her. Stopping for a moment again, he kissed her forehead and then ran kisses down her jaw line to her neck. Amy shut her eyes and relaxed her head back against the pillow. She felt complete. James fully inside her was everything Amy had ever dreamed off.

He bit down hard on her nipple and she screamed out as white-heat pulsated through her body to the core, she was going to come again. James withdrew from her to the tip and she groaned ruefully at the emptiness as the ecstasy she was feeling subdued but rumbled beneath her skin.

"James, I want you back in me." He rocked his hips, teasing her. "James." She shut her eyes and rotated her hips nearer, she needed friction down there.

"There is a word, Amy?" His tone had changed, he was masterfully rasping at her and in control. His words alone were sending quivers shuddering through her body.

"Please. Please?"

She opened her eyes and met the dark carnal circles of his. He was like a man possessed. He was captivated by her. He slammed back into her, and she gasped with pain but absolute delight. He flicked his hips around and withdrew from her again. His pace quickened as he filled her then left her empty. Amy caressed his hair, tugging on the ends every time he hit the sensitive spot inside her. Sweat was glistening on both of their bodies. Amy ran her hands down the back of James' head and neck, and then began to claw her nails into his back in her need to get him even closer. He stopped thrusting, adjusted his position so that his weight was supported on one rippling tricep, grabbed her hands, and held them tightly above her head. James never liked her touching him intimately when naked. She needed to know why, but before she could think anymore he began to thrust again and the pressure within her body built to a final crescendo.

"James, I am coming again."

"Come, Amy."

She did. Amy flew high into the sky as the most intense orgasm she had ever felt pulsated over every inch of her body. Before she could come down again the feeling hit her again.

James groaned out and she knew the tight walls of her pussy were milking his climax from him. They seemed to exist in this state forever, both high and shuddering together. Eventually, James collapsed on her, reached between them, and withdrew from her body. Amy felt empty.

That is when the panic hit her.

The last time this had happened, he had walked out on her. She desperately searched his eyes for signs that he was about to do the same again. She saw none, though, he either wore a very clever mask, or he was as thoroughly sated and happy as she was. He rolled off of her and pulled her into his arms. He was shaking. Amy entangled her arms within his.

"James?" She was worried.

"Did I hurt you?"

She shook her head vehemently.

"No. James. It was unbelievable. I have never, ever, felt that way before. How did you manage to know my body that well? I can't even get a multi orgasm from a vibrator."

He didn't answer her straight away. "You never found the vibrator that was a perfect fit."

She slapped at his chest. He stopped shaking and kissed her.

"I know. I am never going to get rid of this one." The words came out of her mouth before she even realised what she was saying, "I mean...if..." She blushed as he interrupted to spare her embarrassment.

"Well, this one never wants to get rid of its new owner either."

It wasn't a conventional declaration of love.

The front door slammed, and Miranda called out that she was home. The spell between them was broken.

"Mothers have the worst timing."

Amy laughed as James slid from the bed, and she got a last look at his perfect body as he retrieved his jeans from the floor and disappeared into the bathroom. She didn't want to leave the wanton carnality of the sweat-soaked bed. Amy was happy, for the first time since the death of her parents. She felt settled, like she was finally getting her life back.

James was her future.

****

James pulled the condom from his deflating cock, checked it, wrapped it in tissue and tossed it in the bin. He went to the sink and splashed water on his face. He was shaking again. Fuck. What was she doing to him?

He hadn't hurt her. He hadn't hurt her. She had told him that and she seemed so happy. That is what he needed to remember. He loved her so much it was killing him, because he would destroy it. He was vermin. That is why they did to him what they did. James splashed more water on himself. If he could just keep his control, everything would be alright.

CHAPTER FIFTEEN

James

James held Amy's hand tightly as he assisted her to manoeuvre gracefully out of the car in the short skirt she had chosen to wear. He tried not to look at the lissom length of her legs. The press would be waiting and he didn't need to be photographed with a telling bulge in his jeans. A camera picked up everything and the press jumped on it. Matthew and Sonia appeared at their side. Sonia took Amy's bag and they strode purposefully towards the airport with the flashes of cameras going off around them. Why people were interested in his love life, James would never understand. He was, ultimately, a builder. I guess, if you have money, your life becomes public interest, although he had been told on numerous occasions that his looks helped as well.

They breezed through first class check in and were escorted straight through the security check with relative ease, even when Amy set off all the alarms and panicked. James just stood back and laughed as she was searched by the butch security lady. She frowned at him and cuddled a little tighter into him when, instead of going to the first class lounge, they went straight to the plane to board. James had developed the fine art of minimising the waiting times at the airport to the least possible inconvenient length. As much as the lounges were comfortable and well stocked, he just wanted to get on the plane and get travelling. The stewardess greeted them, and they were fast-tracked straight onto the plane and into their comfortable seats.

The seats were private, everyone in first class booked out by his company, so they wouldn't be disturbed. Matthew and Sonia travelled in business class. Usually, he would go with Matthew and not bother with such extravagance but he wanted Amy to himself. James didn't want to make polite conversation with anyone else. He wanted to hold her in his arms while they watched a movie, slept and ate. A stewardess appeared and introduced herself to them, handing them both a glass of champagne and a luxurious gift bag full of toiletries, an eye mask, socks and toothbrush and toothpaste. James looked over to Amy, her eyes were wide with excitement. She had told him before they left for the airport that she had only flown a few times, and never in first class, let alone even in business class; it had always been cheap package flights. She was enjoying the experience. James sat back, closed his eyes and let her converse with the stewardess. It was almost a ten-hour flight to Bangalore, and he had a busy day ahead.

They had been working on developing the hotel for years now, it was a different direction for his firm, a new output. The expansion of business in India meant Bangalore was becoming a vibrant and wealthy city. Many Europeans and Americans were travelling there for business meetings and James himself had done so numerous times for business with his office development branch. He had found the hotels lacking. They had top brands emerging but they were all generic. None of them captured the magic of the country with the modern facilities that a business traveller was expecting. There were one or two authentic, high-class hotels, but their location was not correct. He had managed to secure a prime piece of land and paid attention to the right people to get his planning permission passed easily. As with virtually all government departments he knew, a little cash donation sweetened the path to getting what he wanted. They had worked together with a traditional Indian architect and the hotel was designed as a palace. It was colourful, like the country itself, but not overly so, and the furnishings were luxurious and classy. It had two swimming pools and spa facilities, tennis courts, a fully equipped gymnasium, several different types of restaurants and a whole first-floor wing devoted to branded shops and smaller jewellery shops. The suites all had twenty-four-hour butler service. All staff members had received top class training and would be rewarded for keeping very high standards.

James was looking forward to this trip, the hotel was going to open and months of hard work would come to fruition. But mostly because all the time Amy was going to be at his side to enjoy it all as well. He couldn't be prouder to show her what he did.

The plane sped down the runway and into the air, Amy gripped James' hand tightly. She had also told him earlier that she was nervous of flying. Once in the air, she was okay but the going up and down terrified her. He held her close to his chest and hummed softly to calm her. They must have both actually fallen asleep for a few moments as the air stewardess suddenly appeared at their side with menus and James noticed the seatbelts signs had gone off. Amy studied the menu intently, while he, pretty much knowing what was going to be on it, scanned quickly and made his order. He requested more champagne and flicked through the movie listing. He had seen most of them, so when Amy finally made her order, he pushed the screen away and brought her back into his arms.

"You feeling better?"

"Much. I don't think I have ever fallen asleep on a plane. I was listening to your heartbeat and it just soothed me."

"Glad I could be of assistance. Anything else I can do to make your flight more comfortable Miss Jones?"

Amy looked around the cabin. "You can pass me that blanket; my legs are getting cold."

"Well, if you will wear a ridiculously short skirt..."

"You don't like it?"

"I didn't say that."

The stewardess brought them their dinner and they chatted a little bit more about the hotel and what they would be doing in India. James could see that Amy was a little bit worried about the full schedule but when he told her that, after the opening, he had booked for them to go to the Maldives for a week she was stunned into silence.

"You didn't have to do that."

"I wanted another holiday."

"James, the holiday to Lanzarote was the first one you had taken in years. And now another one in just a few short months. People will think you have gone crazy and are having an early mid-life crisis."

"Maybe I have." He raised a playful eyebrow at her and slid his hand further up her leg. When they were in the Maldives, she was going to spend the entire time naked if he had his way. Amy leant into him and whispered into his ear.

"So, the bathroom in this cabin. Is it ours alone?"

"Yes, Amy. Why?"

"I think I need to visit it. Do you want to join me?" She winked. Was she suggesting what he thought she was suggesting? His jeans suddenly felt decidedly snug. No. He needed to keep their sexual liaisons to a bed. Since the other night, they had been together several times but always in bed. He was better able to control himself that way. He wouldn't hurt her that way.

"I am not sure that is a good idea, Amy."

Her face fell, "You don't want to? Would we get into trouble? I thought that is why we have first class to ourselves."

Damn. He had shot himself in the foot there. One time wouldn't hurt. He held his hand out to Amy and stood to follow her. The stewardess poked her head around the curtain, saw Amy kiss him, and quickly shut it again. They would be the talk of the crew by the time they emerged from the toilet, but he didn't care. Amy was all that James ever wanted and any opportunity he got to be inside her he was going to take it.

He closed the door after them and locked it. Amy was already removing her tiny pants.

"I only have one spare in my hand luggage so I don't want you ripping these ones." She laughed and put them by the sink. He pulled her close and they kissed, mouths tangling in an unspoken urgent need. They had had sex before coming to the airport but they both still wanted more. He ran a hand down her body and under her skirt to prepare her for him to enter her but was surprised when he found her pussy dripping already.

"How long have you been like that?"

"Since we left the apartment."

She blushed.

"But we had only just..."

"I know. But I hadn't seen you in such tight jeans before." She ran her hands around to his backside and gave it a little squeeze. "I like the way your arse looks in them."

"You are a bad, bad girl, Amy."

"Punish me then?"

He pulled back and opened his jeans, pushing them half way down his legs. His magnificently erect cock proudly leapt towards Amy's erotic scent.

"Shit. I don't have a condom. They're in my wallet." He went to pull his jeans back up, hoping that he would be able to get his dick back in them.

"No worries." He looked at her, confused, and she pulled one from her skirt pocket. "I am always prepared."

"How many more days do we have to be careful?"

"Five."

"Stock up."

She laughed and he took the condom from her and put it on.

She braced herself against the sink, with one foot on the toilet, and displayed herself to him. The toilet was a tight squeeze, but he got himself close and thrust, without warning, into her. She gasped and clamped down on his cock. Fuck she was so tight. He felt every undulation of her muscles and when they massaged him, he struggled to keep his control. This wasn't going to be a sensual lovemaking. It was going to be raw and animalistic. He pulled out and rapidly thrust back in again, he repeated this till he found his rhythm. Amy placed her hand on his neck, she looked at him to see that this was alright. He was conscious that whenever they made love he refused to have her touch him when he was naked. James still had his shirt on however and she wouldn't be able to get at his flesh. He gave her a small nod and Amy let her head fall back, her eyes fluttered shut and she became lost in what he was doing to her.

All around him came the noises of the stewardesses in business class looking after their guests. James wondered if they could hear him every time he slammed into Amy and knocked her further back against the sink. He wondered if they could hear every cry of lust she made when he swirled his hips before he pulled back out again. James' legs began to quiver. This was too good. He was struggling to maintain his control. The fact that he was pleasuring the woman he loved in a place where anybody could hear them or realise what they were doing was sending him over the edge. His balls drew up tight, he was ready to unload within Amy, but he needed to hear her come first.

"Amy, touch yourself. Make yourself come for me."

Her head snapped up, her eyes opened and her hand instantly went between her legs and sought out her sensitive clit.

Fuck, when they were in a place with more room he needed to get her to do all kind of things to herself. She obeyed him so freely. He needed to be able to watch her pleasure herself, see her own fingers slip in her wet pussy, coat them with her juices, and he would make her suck them afterwards. Know what she tastes like. He shut his eyes tight. It was already starting-- he was imagining things.

Amy screamed out when she came. He clapped a hand over her mouth to silence her as he released deep inside her. Their movements stilled and he withdrew and brought her into his arms. They were both brcathless, and he would need a shower as soon as they got to the hotel. Maybe Amy would join him. He quickly shook that thought from his head. He didn't need to get excited again. In bed, James. You can only do it with Amy in bed. You can't risk losing her now.

"We better get back to our seats. I am sure the crew is talking already."

"You think so? Will they be angry?"

"Matthew will have given them a tip to keep quiet."

"Seriously? Have you done it for all the girls you have flown with? Or did you plan this before we boarded?"

"Neither." He pulled up his jeans and disposed of the evidence. He pulled the freshly laid out wash cloth and wet it before running it over Amy's pussy to clean it. She didn't push him away but he got the feeling she was angry at him now. "Amy, you aren't the only one that just got inducted into the mile-high club. I promise you, Matthew just does these things. It is why I pay him so well. I didn't plan this. If you remember rightly, you were the one that suggested it. And to clarify, I have never had sex with someone on a plane until now."

She pulled her skirt back down and smoothed it before putting her knickers back on.

"Sorry." She put her arms around him, "I got jealous then."

"I like it, shows how much what we just did means to you."

A knock came to the door.

"Yes." he answered sternly.

"Um, Sir. Sorry. The Captain says we are about to hit a patch of turbulence and that he will need to switch on the seatbelt sign. You will need to return to your seats at once."

Amy tried to suppress a giggle at the unease in the stewardess' voice.

"She probably thinks you will take the tip back because she interrupted us."

James laughed and opened the door to the flushed face of the stewardess.

"It is alright. We will return. I think my girlfriend is feeling much better now. She is a terribly nervous flyer."

The seat belt sign flashed on and James helped Amy

back to her seat, did her belt up, and then lowered her chair to a fully reclined bed. He got into the seat next to her and did the same with his. They both lay on their sides staring at each other in silence as the first bumps came. The lights in the cabin switched off. The next thing James knew they were being woken for breakfast, and it was forty-five minutes until landing.

CHAPTER SIXTEEN

Amy

They were met at the airport by an Indian man, who was introduced to Amy as Naresh, their driver for the duration of the stay. She queried why Matthew wasn't driving as normal and was told that driving in India was completely different to the UK and that it was better left to those that knew the rules of the road. She quickly learnt what this meant on the hour-long trip from the airport to the hotel. Despite the fact that it was six in the morning and the roads were what she deemed to be country roads marked with potholes, they were busy. People walked wherever they wanted. Bikes, laden with whole families at times, zoomed around the car, green and yellow took-tooks (Indian rickshaws) full to busting of people and goods turned with a moment's notice and they even had to stop for five minutes while a cow crossed the road and was worshipped by locals. Amy stared wide eyed out the window all the time, she was taking everything in that this strange city had to offer. James held her hand and laid back and closed his eyes again. He had seen it all before and nothing felt alien to him. They entered the district of Whitefield, the driver was giving her a bit of a running commentary on points of interest, and the city turned more into what she had expected, high-rise office buildings and malls devoted to drawing the Western visitors into spending their abundance of money. All the companies' buildings had their names on them and she recognised a lot. They pulled into the driveway of a hotel that she saw was called The Malu Palace and the car stopped. Security guards appeared and placed a mirror under the front and rear of the car. They then opened all the doors so that a security dog could sniff within the car. Amy looked at

James in concern.

"It is standard procedure everywhere. You will get used it. It makes you feel safer in the end."

The security guard didn't speak to her but smiled and shut the door.

It was 7 am Indian time, 1:30 am UK time when they pulled up outside of the hotel and the doors were opened by traditionally dressed porters. All Amy wanted was to have a shower and sleep for another couple of hours but she needed to support James. Sonia took her bag and pointed to a scanner. Amy nodded. Security was tight in this country. But James was right, it did make her feel safe. Or maybe that was the fact James had barely let go of her hand since they left London. She could feel people looking at her, and she didn't know whether it was because she was James' girl-friend, the fact she had a next-to-nothing skirt on, when everyone else was covered, or the fact she was blonde and most people here were dark.

They entered the lobby of the hotel and the manager greeted James. James let go of her hand. Two young girls came over and bowed before her and wished her *Namaste*, something she had been told meant hello. She responded in kind and they placed a flower garland over her head and then blessed her with a red-painted bindi to her forehead. James was having the same done to him, as were Matthew and Sonia, the former not looking that impressed with the garland. Another girl brought them a cloth to wipe their hands and a fourth presented them with a drink in a coco-nut shell.

"What is it?" Amy whispered to Sonia.

"Coconut water."

"Is it nice?"

"I like it, some don't."

Amy took a little sip. It tasted quite sour but she liked it, it was refreshing and despite being 7 am it was hot outside already.

"Thank you." She said to the girls and they scurried

away. James called Amy to his side,

"Raji, this is my girlfriend, Amy Jones. She will be accompanying me to all the opening ceremony events. We will need to get her a sari made for the grand opening on Friday."

Raji shook his head like he was saying no then held his hand out to Amy and she shook it,

"Nice to meet you, Miss Jones. I am Raji, the hotel manager. Anything you need, just ask. Mr North I will have my wife personally escort Miss Jones to the city today to source a Sari. I know just the shop."

Amy looked at him confused. "But didn't you just shake your head to say no?"

James laughed out loud, Amy turned and glared at him.

"In India, Amy when a person shakes their head like that, it means yes."

"Really."

James nodded his head in demonstration and Raji laughed this time,

"Except we don't look as silly as Mr North doing so."

"He just looks like a nodding dog."

James frowned at Amy.

"No more encouraging Amy to tease me, Raji, she is perfectly capable on her own." He chuckled.

"I think I like your girlfriend, Mr North. Come, let me show you to your suite. I have put Mr Kumar and his entourage in the presidential suite. I hope that is alright. You have the second best rooms in the hotel."

"Makes sense to me." James motioning for him to lead the way.

Amy caught up with James and held his hand again.

"Who is Mr Kumar?"

"He is one of the most famous Bollywood stars. He is officially opening the hotel for us."

"That is nice."

"He is being paid well to do it."

"Oh."

"It is all good publicity, Amy."

"Maybe he can get someone to teach me Bollywood dancing. It has always looked fun."

James didn't answer that statement as Raji began talking to him again.

The lobby of the hotel was vast, it had ornate carvings all over it and displays of exotic flowers on plinths. Staff bustled around cleaning everything. Amy didn't know why-- the place looked spotless to her. The lift was decked in beautiful pale marble that matched the floors of the hotel. Raji opened the door to their suite and James ushered her in. She stood there amazed. The walls were adorned with exquisite carvings and artwork and the fabrics were the finest hand printed silks. This was just the entrance hall to their suite, doors lead off into a huge lounge area with a separate working area to the right. To the far end were two further rooms which she guessed must be for Matthew and Sonia. Their ensuite was the size of her flat back in Kennington. She was scared to even open the door to the bedroom she would share with James but eventually found the courage. It took her breath away. The marble flooring ending halfway to the bed and was replaced with what were hand-made carpets. The bed itself was the size of two double beds pushed together but it was only one because it was four posted and bedecked in the most fabulous silk fabrics. The tables, wardrobes and television units were hand carved from wood. Amy had tears in her eyes because she was somewhere so beautiful and that it was all because of a vision that James had had and seen through to fruition.

James appeared behind her and wrapped his hands around her waist.

"Do you like it? Do you think it is too much?"

"It is so beautiful, James. I feel like I am in paradise."

"All of the furnishings and fabrics have been sourced from within India, and the contracts have gone to families where it would make a complete difference to their lives."

Tears started to tumble down her cheeks now.

"I love you."

He turned her around in his arms.

"What?"

"I love you."

"I love you as well, Amy."

All Amy wanted to do was take James into that big bed and spend the rest of the day with him there, but he had business meetings and she didn't want to be a distraction to him. She wiped her tears of happiness away.

"You go shower and I will unpack. You need to get all your work done so we can have a dinner in the roof top restaurant tonight."

"I will look forward to that all day Miss Jones."

"Go."

James disappeared into the bathroom and Amy began to unpack the suitcases which had appeared in the room as if by magic. She took his toiletry bag to him just as he stepped into the shower. Amy wanted to join him, but she had to be sensible and not distract him. He was here for work and not romance. There would be time for that when they went to the Maldives. Oh, my god, she was going to the Maldives. She tried not to let out a little whoop of joy.

Amy left the bathroom with a final quick look at James' sculpted body and went back to the bedroom. She still felt so tired despite the fact they had slept for a few hours. She took her clothes off and tossed them into the linen bin provided. Part of the duties of the butler was to ensure that all their clothes were washed, ironed and returned. This was truly unlike any hotel she had ever stayed in before. She slipped a tiny nightdress over her head and got between the sheets. She should shower, but she just wanted to rest her eyes until James had finished in the bathroom.

The next thing she knew the phone next to the bed was ringing.

"Hello?" she picked it up and sleepily spoke.

"Miss Jones? *Namaste*, I am Ratu, Raji's wife. He has asked me to escort you to choose a sari. Is now convenient?"

She sat bolt upright in the bed.

"What time is it?"

"It is midday, Miss."

"Midday. Oh. I am sorry. I have been sleeping." She looked over to the pillow and saw James had placed a little note on his pillow and a lotus flower. "Could you give me half an hour?"

"Of course Miss, I will meet you in reception."

"Thank you so much."

Amy picked up the note and read the declaration of love from James and his promises for the evening. She placed it in her bag. Next, she got out of the bed, stripped the nightdress from her body and jumped into the shower. In half an hour on the dot, she was in reception, she had dressed in a long maxi dress and had a shawl draped around her shoulders. She had been told that, in the city, it was best not draw attention to your flesh. Ratu greeted her with a firm handshake and a nod of the head. She was dressed in Indian attire; an outfit Amy learned was called a *salwar kameez*. She had gold bracelets all up her wrists, numerous piercings in her ears, and a jewelled bindi in the middle of her head. Amy was informed that they were going to the city to a place called Commercial Street. It was one of the main shopping streets in Bangalore and was something that she needed to experience. Sonia appeared at her side as they got into the car and presented her with a bottle of water.

"You will need this, Miss Jones. It will be hot out there."

Sonia was right, as they got out of the air-conditioned car, the heat hit Amy. It was early afternoon in the middle of the country's summer. The temperature must have been hitting 35 degrees or more in the shade. She was instantly sweating as they walked up the steps to the store. Ratu had another bag with her and this was taken away and placed into a security locker. Their handbags were searched. Again she was reassured that this was all normal.

When they entered the store, it was like she had walked

into a rainbow, a sparkly one, as well, as everything seemed to be embedded with beads and gems. People milled everywhere, Ratu explained that most of them were staff and that, on a busy weekend, the store could almost be impossible to move in. Amy didn't know how anyone could actually shop in somewhere like this. A friendly gentlemen greeted them in perfect English and when Ratu explained what they needed, Amy was ushered to one side of the room and provided with a seat. A drink was brought to her--coconut water again--and two ladies began to question her on her favourite colours.

"She was a bit overwhelmed by it all.

They turned to the walls which were covered from top to bottom with fabrics and pulled out several blues.

"Light or dark, Madame?"

"I like the darker ones."

"Good choice, Madame."

"This one?" The other lady spoke and held up an aquamarine length of fabric with embellishments that Amy thought looked like millions of sequins.

"A bit darker?"

The other lady held up a sapphire-coloured one this time. This had beads sewn onto it in patterns.

"This is hand sewn, Madame."

"Matches your skin and hair perfectly."

Amy looked to Ratu for help.

"Why don't you try it on, Miss?"

"I don't know how to wear one."

"Stand up please, Madame."

Amy did as instructed. One of the girls took her shawl away. It was neatly folded and placed beside her. The other showed her how to stand and in what seemed like a fluid movement the sari was wrapped around her with ease. A mirror was brought and Amy stood before it looking at her reflection. She loved it. It suited her colour perfectly. James would like it.

"How much?"

Ratu interjected. "Mr North has taken care of it, Miss."

"Of course." she couldn't be angry at him; she had expected it. "But I would still like to know the cost."

Ratu looked at the girls and they said something between them in the regional dialogue. "It is around two hundred pounds in your money, Miss."

Amy gasped.

"It is hand sewn in the finest silks."

"Oh."

"Mr North will love you in it. He stated that cost was not an issue."

"He would." she smirked, she was going to let him get away with it this time though as she absolutely loved the sari. "We will take it."

The sale was run up before Amy could change her mind. She thanked the staff and they returned to the car. Amy was told that usually they would take the Sari to a shop nearby to choose fabric for the underskirt and lining, it would then be taken to a seamstress to complete the work, but Ratu would arrange all of that without the need to impose on her time even more.

Amy was hungry. She hadn't eaten since they had had breakfast on the plane. Ratu made instructions to the driver and they pulled up next to a well-known fast food restaurant. Amy sighed. She really didn't fancy a burger.

"Is there not something different?"

Ratu looked out the window. "Oh no Miss, we are not going there. The restaurant is on the other side."

Amy turned her head and looked at a restaurant that said Veg Only. It didn't look anything special, in fact, it looked like a cheap diner when they entered. They were shown to a seat and Amy ordered a lemonade and allowed Ratu to order the food as most of the menu wasn't in English.

"I haven't ordered you much, Mr North has a big dinner planned tonight so you don't want to be full up."

The food arrived really quickly and the lemonade Amy

had ordered turned out to be a proper lemonade. Ratu told her that in India if you wanted lemonade like in the UK you needed to order the brand. Amy stored that bit of information for the future but still enjoyed the proper lemonade. The meal consisted of vegetables only.

"Many of the people in India are vegetarian."

"I don't mind; you will just have to tell me what some of the food is."

"These are *chapatti*, Indian bread and this is *gobi manchurian*, it is spicy cauliflower, and this is *paneer masala* which is Indian cheese in a butter gravy and the final one is a *dahl*, which is lentils infused with spices."

Amy sampled all the dishes, thoroughly enjoyed them, and even ordered some *gobi manchurian* to take back to James.

By the time they got back to the hotel, it was getting late, and Amy found James asleep. She stood there for a few moments watching him as he slept. He was sprawled out naked on the bed with only a thin sheet covering him. He really was the most handsome man she had ever known. He must have been exhausted. His clothes where just strewn upon the floor. His back faced her. She had never had a chance to have a proper look at the tattoo on his back. It was very intricate in its detail. The wings of the angel circled his shoulder blades and in the middle sat the figure of the man. She had never noticed before the sad expression on the angel's face. Tentatively she reached out to touch it lightly. She wanted to wipe away the tears she imagined it was crying. The skin underneath felt different. She leant in for a closer look and saw that his back was marred with ugly scarring. The tattoo was hiding it all.

James stirred in the bed. She stood back, and he turned to face her.

"Hello beautiful. When did you get back?"

"Just now." She smiled.

"What is the time?"

"Just after 6."

"Good." He pulled her towards him, "Just time to christen this big bed."

Amy wanted to ask him about the scars but now wasn't the time. Instead, she pulled her dress over her head and climbed into the bed next to him.

CHAPTER SEVENTEEN

James

"Make sure that you check all the rooms, and personally. I am not leaving anything to chance. They all need to have one of the gift bags in them." James ran his hand through his hair. "And the press packs. Make sure they're all laid out in preparation as well. I am trusting you Raji." Amy appeared at James' side and handed him a glass of water with ice and a slice of lemon. Raji nodded and hurried away.

"You need to come and have an hour's rest. I will help Raji check the rooms."

"I don't have time for a rest Amy." He snapped at her, "the hotel's opening is in four hours, and there is still so much left to do." He was distracted by two waiters laying a table out incorrectly and started for them, his fists clenched. Amy jumped in front of him.

"Bedroom now." She stood with her hands on her hips and lips pursed together in defiance. "You will do as you are told. I will sort the tables and check the rooms. You have barely sat down or slept in three days. If you don't rest now, you will collapse during the opening. And *that* will be the headline news, and not the hotel." James tried to walk around her, he really didn't have time for this but she continued to block his path. "James, please. Listen to me."

He could see the worry in her eyes as she looked up at him. He drew her to him and cuddled her.

"I am sorry. You are right. Let me just sort the table, Raji will sort the rooms and then you can come and keep me company while I rest?"

"Alright. But if I join you in the bedroom James, no sex. Deal."

"Deal." He couldn't be bothered to argue. James sorted

the table layout and then virtually dragged Amy to their suite. Matthew was there cleaning his shoes for the evening. Sonia was watching television and grumbling at the poor choices of channels. James instantly vowed to rectify that, he didn't want anyone to find any faults. Amy led him into the bedroom, shut the door, took his jacket and shirt off, helped him on the bed, and removed his shoes and socks. He lay on the pillow and instantly relaxed. He tapped the bed for her to come and lay next to him. She shook her head.

"No, James. Shut your eyes and sleep."

"Amy, at least lay down with me."

"No."

"Seriously?"

"You can't always have your own way, James."

"Why not?"

"Because I said so. Shut your eyes and sleep."

"Yeah. That is going to be a little difficult." He looked down at the rapidly expanding tent in his trousers.

"You are insatiable."

"You are incredibly sexy." She had forced him to rest, but he wasn't going to allow her to win. He needed to take it back. "Remove all your clothes, Amy."

"No." She folded her arms at him in a challenge. His cock jumped and he gripped the bed to maintain his dwindling restraint. God, she loved to test him. He slid slowly from the bed and lowered his trousers so his erect cock jutted out straight towards her.

"Are you really going to leave me like this?" He prayed the answer that she gave wouldn't be no.

"I am not going touch you, James. I told you that." She turned away from him and his mouth dropped open. He had never had a woman defy him likc this. He looked down at his hands. They were shaking.

"Amy. Come here and suck me, or I will put you over this bed and spank your arse until it is red." The words had left his mouth before he had a chance to think. What was she doing to him? He was losing it.

She turned back around and she had undone the buttons at the front of her knee length dress. She slipped the dress to the floor. He met her eyes, which were still full of defiance. What was she doing?

"I won't be sucking you, I won't be touching you. If you want to come, you will have to do it yourself."

"What?" His answer came out in a strangled moan of longing. Her bra followed the dress to the floor. He reached out to touch her breasts but she smacked his hand away.

"You don't touch me, either."

"Amy come on, enough is enough. Stop fooling around."

"I am not." She walked over to the chair in the corner of the room and sat on it. She parted her legs and brought one foot up onto the seat. His blackening eyes followed the path of her hand as she trailed it over her breasts and down to the cleft between her legs. She pulled the flimsy material of her pants across and displayed herself to him--she was glistening with dewy moisture. He hissed and his hand grabbed hold of his cock and began to stroke it. What in the hell was she doing to him? James watched as she used one hand to hold her delicate folds apart and with the other, ran a finger down in between them and circled her clit, massaging and teasing it. He tugged harder on his cock, groaning with each stroke around the head. His eyes flicked to Amy's. She was mesmerised by the way he played with himself.

She lowered her middle finger and stuck it within herself. James wiped away the bead of pre-cum that appeared on his cock. Amy was writhing against her finger, she put another one in and then let go of her folds and began to massage her clit again.

James had dreamt of this moment. He couldn't believe it was happening. It shouldn't happen. This was wrong, wasn't it?

He had no control. It was all Amy. It wasn't in bed. It was erotic, and he was more turned on than he knew. Fuck, he was losing his mind. He was a pervert. That's what they had called him. He had the scars.

Amy moaned.

"James, I am going to come. Are you close? I want us to come together."

"Yes." Was all he managed before he violently came into his hand. His legs began to quiver as Amy cried out with her own release. He tried to focus on her, but his head was swirling, his cock was still pumping what seemed like an endless swathe of essence into his hand. His legs gave way and he collapsed onto the bed. James couldn't move, he could barely catch a breath.

That had actually just happened. He caught, out of the corner of his eye, Amy lowering her legs and get up from the chair. She fetched tissues from the box on the dressing table and he watched as she wiped his hand. No. No. She shouldn't be doing this. His mind was endlessly twisting, his heart beating so rapidly he thought it would explode.

He was heading down the dark path again. He was going to lose her. He was forcing her to do his dirty stuff. Amy sat beside him on the bed. She kissed his now sweating fore-head. He needed air.

"I am sorry." He pulled up his trousers, and without looking back, ran from the room. He was shirtless and bare-foot, but he needed to put distance between them. He heard Amy call after him but he couldn't stop. The roof was the nearest place. He needed to breathe. He was struggling. He couldn't find any air. He hurtled up the fire escape exit and burst into the roof. Gulping, he tried to get as much air into his lungs as possible. He didn't hear the footsteps behind him until the last minute.

"You can't hide the truth from her any longer."

He spun around. Matthew stood before him.

"Leave me alone."

"No, James. Whatever that bitch did to you, Amy differ-ent. She loves you and I think, even though you are trying to hide it, she is exactly the same as you."

"She will hate me. I can't see that happen. I love her."

"She will hate you if you keep walking out on her like this." Matthew reached out and grabbed his arm. "Go talk to her."

"Fuck you, Matthew. You don't know anything." James took a swing at him to try and shake him off but his body-guard ducked. James turned again and caught him hard on the side of the face. Matthew reciprocated and pushed him hard against the wall. His back stung as it hit the rigid sur-face, the scars beneath his tattoo instantly burned. He tried to push Matthew off him but the bodyguard was too well trained and too strong.

"I took you to the hospital that night James. I stayed with you until your mother could get there and remained in the waiting room for hours after. Don't tell me I don't know an-ything. I couldn't get to you in time then to save you but I am not going to let you make the biggest mistake of your life here and now. Because if you continue down this path than that is what it will be."

"She will hate me." He sent a pounding blow into his bodyguard's stomach but his own hand came off worse against the steely abs he found there.

"Did she hate you during whatever you just did that trig-gered this off?" James froze. "She is in your room crying right now. Wondering what she has done to upset you."

"She didn't leave?"

"No, you idiot." James relaxed into Matthew's grip and the bodyguard let go. "Sonia is in there consoling her."

"Fuck." James screamed at the top of his voice and a flock of pigeons that had been quietly nesting nearby cas-caded into the sky below the rooftop. "I need to solve this don't I?"

"Yes. You let her go and you are on your own. I will quit."

A cough came from behind them. It was Sonia.

"I am sorry Sir, Mr Raji is looking for you urgently. The press is showing up already and several of the guests as well."

James slouched against the wall.

"Amy?"

"Mrs Ratu is with her helping her dress and makeup."

"Stay with her, but tell her as soon as this opening is all over, I will explain everything to her. And Sonia, tell her I love her." He turned back to Matthew. "Go get me my suit. I will change in your room."

Matthew nodded and disappeared with Sonia back down the stairs.

James stood on the rooftop breathing in what he could of the city 'fresh air'. He thought his past had been just that, the past. James thought he could suppress it and hide it but if he was to save his relationship with Amy, there was the one big demon he needed to face. He would get through this evening and, tomorrow, he would tell her everything and she would be able to make her own decisions about him and whether she wanted to stay with him or not.

He just prayed that she did.

CHAPTER EIGHTEEN

Amy

The door opened and all the guests filled into the elegant ballroom. Amy stood at James' side ready to greet them. Raji and his wife were with them, along with several executives including James' Indian and UK-based Architects. Amy followed Ratu's lead and presented a little curtsey to everyone rather than a handshake. She didn't need to speak to them; woman were merely a decoration for their men in Indian culture. She didn't mind tonight. Her head, with everything that had happened earlier, was all over the place. A smile was about all she could manage.

Amy felt like a princess in her sari. She had had her long blonde hair pulled up into a fancy hair style that was decorated with delicate jewelled pins. Her makeup had been done for her and the hotel had loaned her gold bracelets so numerous that they covered her wrists and forearms. She even had a bindi on her forehead. It was a beautiful sapphire colour to match those on her sari. James was dressed in a jodhpur suit. His jacket was a special Indian design similar to the hotel's logo, blue and gold in colour. Ratu was dressed the same and Amy just knew that the suits had been specially made for them because they fitted each man like a second skin. After the final few guests shuffled through the welcoming committee, James took Amy's hand and lead her to their table for the Indian banquet. She could tell he was nervous; his palms were sweaty. She whispered quietly to him as they walked,

"You are doing well. Everybody looks happy."

He smiled down at her, "I love you. I am sorry, Amy. I wish I didn't have to do this now. I owe you an explanation."

"I love you too, James. Please, forget that for now. I am here to support you. You have worked so hard for this." James pulled her seat out as they reached their table. "Tomorrow we can talk. Tonight we celebrate." She leant up and kissed him.

"Thank you." All the gentlemen stood as the ladies took their seats and then they sat. Amy sat next to James and the Bollywood star, Mr Kumar, and next to him was the most beautiful woman Amy had ever seen. Her jet black hair was as elaborately decorated as Amy's and her hands were covered in mehndi designs. They were beautiful and intricate. The starter was brought, a mixture of *pakoras*. These were pieces of vegetables deep fried in garam flour. The sauce served with it was incredible. Champagne was flowing and while James chatted to one of his big investors on his left, Amy engaged in conversation with Mr Kumar and his wife, Meena. They had met on the set of a film where she played his love interest and married after a whirlwind romance. They had three children, though the woman didn't look as though she had ever been pregnant.

When Amy had told them about the fact that she used to dance in England, she didn't divulge where, but they had promised to show her how to do some of the Bollywood dancing later. Amy was so excited.

The main course was brought, for most people this consisted of a vegetable biryani but if you wanted you had the option to have a chicken one instead. Amy opted for chicken and found it really alien that you had to opt for meat. James told her that unlike England, meat was the opt in here. Animals were sacred and worshipped. She would never actually find beef to eat as well due to the cow being the most sacred animal. She wondered about fish, cheese and eggs. James laughed and told her not to mention eggs. A lot of people didn't eat them either because of where they came from.

It had been a nightmare for his chefs to decide on a dessert. The Indians didn't overly do desserts but he had wanted it because it would be what his travelling guests wished, but they had struggled with simple things such as flour, it was differently made in India so they had had to import a load. Amy squeezed his leg under the table. Dinner was cleared away, the speeches started. James and Mr Kumar took centre stage and Amy proudly clapped loudly as they officially declared the hotel open and cut a ribbon. Amy could visibly see James relax as the ribbon was cut and everyone cheered. He had done it.

The live band started, and Meena begged Amy to join her as some lively Indian music struck up. Amy stood beside the dance floor and removed her high heeled shoes at Meena's direction. Meena demonstrated a couple of necessary steps. As soon as she realised Amy could pick up dance as they did it, she launched fully into a proper Bollywood dance. Amy followed her, and the crowd cleared a part of the dance floor for them. They were clapping as Meena performed the dance and Amy followed her movements a few seconds later. Amy was smiling so much her cheeks were hurting, she wasn't quite sure how she was keeping the sari on as she danced but it seemed to be staying in place. Mr Kumar joined them and performed the moves with them. Everybody stopped what they were doing and watched them. A big finish came to the dance which saw first Meena and then Amy twirled in the air by Mr. Kumar. The band stopped playing and everyone cheered. Amy was sure she must have looked a sweaty mess but she didn't care. Through the haze of faces, she saw James watching her. He had the biggest smile on his face and he was clapping so hard she thought he must be hurting his hands. She curtsied to the group, left the dance floor, and went straight to his arms. He embraced her and pressed a kiss to the top of her head.

" I didn't know you could dance like that."

"I have been dancing since I was four. I just always picked it up really easily. I miss it in some ways. I will have to dance more for you." She giggled and then realised what she had said. "I am sorry."

"No, don't be. I want you to dance for me. You can teach me as well. I have two left feet." He laughed. "Maybe something a bit less energetic for a start, though. I always fancied learning the tango."

"I think I could oblige you there."

They stayed at each other's side for the rest of the evening. Stalls had been laid out selling different products from the country and one even did mehndi which Amy dragged James to. He refused to get any done, saying it was for girls despite the fact Raji had it all over his hands. However, he helped Amy pick out a winding pattern that snaked down her forearm, over her hand and down her middle finger. It reminded her of his tattoo. She loved it and actually told him she was going to consider getting it done permanently. James whispered into her ear. "You do that, and I won't be responsible for how hard you make me." She reached out with her painted hand and stroked it down his face.

It was two in the morning by the time the final few guests made their way to their bedrooms, Amy was almost dead on her feet. The staff busied themselves, changing around settings so that the banquet room would be ready for a buffet breakfast the next morning. The evening had been about Indian food but the breakfast would be a traditional European affair.

Amy couldn't remember where, but she had lost her shoes somewhere around midnight. She was tiny now when she stood next to James, though he still used her as a leaning post to say goodnight to the final guest.

"Come on you. Time for bed."

Amy could barely keep her eyes open as they headed for the lift. James scooped her into his arms and carried her from the lift to their suite. Matthew opened the door and bid them good night. James placed Amy on their bed and as she sat there dozily aware of what was happening, he removed the pins from her hair and brushed it out. He next helped her to remove her sari and guided her, naked, into the bathroom. He waited outside, and when she emerged he had undressed. He reached behind his back, produced her nightgown, and put it over her head. He then led her to the bed and laid her down and covered her up with the sheet. She waited for him to kiss her but he didn't. He just went to the bathroom without a word. What was he doing? Amy was baffled. When he came out, he climbed into the bed beside her and brought her into his arms. He kissed her on the forehead and whispered, "Goodnight."

She responded in kind and he turned out the lights. Amy lay there in the dark, suddenly wide awake. She was in bed with a man that she knew held a secret from her. One that made him terrified of her when they made love in any way that wasn't vanilla sex. He had run out on her twice now. He was going to tell her but she didn't think she could sleep before he did. James groaned, was he asleep or like her thinking. She turned in his arms and sat up to reach a bottle of water beside her bed. She had had a few drinks that night but not many. She certainly wasn't drunk and she knew James wasn't either. She took a sip and when she turned back to lay down.

James had rolled over so his back was facing her. The wings of the angel were caught in a flicker of moonlight that streaked through the drapes.

She reached out, the tip of her finger millimetres from the tattoo and the scars she had seen hidden underneath. He turned in the bed and looked up at her with his sorrow-filled eyes.

"James, what you have to tell me. Does it have anything to do with your tattoos and the scars they hide?"

CHAPTER NINETEEN

James

James' world fell apart at Amy's words. She knew. She had seen them. He had always been so careful to make sure they were covered in full light. You had to get so close to study them and see the scars. She couldn't have seen them in this light. "How?" Had Matthew told her?

"The first night we got here when I returned from shopping. It was still daylight and you were sleeping in the bed. You have never let me look at the tattoos properly. I wanted to."

"Are you horrified?"

He sat up next to her and she brought her hand to his stubbled face. "No. I want to know how you got hurt. Is it related to why you ran from me?"

"I don't want to lose you, Amy."

"James, I know we were going to do this tomorrow, but I think you need to talk to me now. I need to know what happened to you."

He nodded, reached over and took a sip of water. He was shaking, he was so scared. She was going to walk out on him her and now and he would never see her again. He owed her an explanation, though.

"Please hear the whole story, Amy, before you say anything. Before you make your mind up about me. Please, will you promise me that?"

"Of course." She moved her hand down to his and squeezed it with reassurance.

"I told you I had a girlfriend, and we broke up about five years ago. Our split was not amicable. In fact, it was completely the opposite. By the end, she despised me. We had been together since we were 16. Our relationship didn't become physical until we had been together for four years. She was very religious and wanted to save herself until she was sure I was the right one. I wasn't ready for marriage, though. I wanted to build my company first. Eventually, and I didn't pressure her, she decided that I was the one and we consummated our relationship." He saw Amy wince. "Her view of sex, though, differed from mine. She believed anything that wasn't the missionary position was wrong. Eventually, I began to find it hard to get off during sex with her. I loved her, though or well I thought I did. So I suggested different positions, and she would punish me and deny me sex for weeks. We would argue about it a lot. I was masturbating more than being with her. I used to enjoy going away on trips because it meant I could stick on a porn video and wank to it. One night I decided that I needed to do something or our relationship was going to fall apart. I brought her a blindfold."

"What did she say?"

"She agreed to try it. I tied it around her eyes and we started to...you know." Amy winced again.

"I know."

"Except I got carried away. I flipped her over and went to enter her from behind. I smacked her arse. I was so erect, I thought I was going to come then and there. It felt so good. So freeing. I wanted more. I pushed into her and she screamed. She scrambled away, ripped the blindfold from her face, and called me the devil. She quickly dressed and left the house. I tried to see her the next day but she refused. Her brothers told me I was unholy and a freak. I was never to go near their sister again. They wanted compensation for her suffering. She felt like a whore. She would need counselling for life, and the odds of her being able to form another relationship were slim to none. I had to give them money. I was already a millionaire but it nearly bankrupted the company. If I hadn't paid them they would have gone to the press and sold stories about me." He stopped and drew breath. He had spoken so fast he wanted to make sure Amy had taken everything in. "Do you understand everything?" She looked at him blankly or in shock. He really couldn't decide. "Amy?"

"They made you pay compensation to your girlfriend of five years because you tried to have sex with her doggy style?"

"Yes."

Her tiny fists were tightly clenched. She was angry. No, she was seething. She thought he was sick as well.

"That doesn't explain the scars."

"You sure you want to hear that bit?"

"James, I want to hear everything."

"I didn't want another girlfriend after that. I thought I would just throw myself into the business. I watched porn and BDSM videos to satisfy my needs. One night I was passing a club, I went in and found a sub for the evening, and she did things. Things the way I wanted them. The way I had seen them on the videos. After that, I visited her on other occasions."

Amy interrupted.

"What sort of things?"

"I tied her up. I whipped her, we used toys" he paused and looked away. "We masturbated in front of each other." She inhaled sharply. He really was a disgusting freak. She would hate him.

"Is that how you got the scars? Did she go too far?"

"No. One night I was leaving the club. I had sent Matthew to get the car. I had had a little too much to drink and wandered into a nearby park. My ex-girlfriend's brothers were walking home and saw me. They knew what the club did. They saw a way to make money; except the first time I had drawn up a watertight contract. I refused. A fight started. Two against one, and the one wasn't entirely sober. I was outnumbered. They got me on the floor. They took my belt from my jeans and hit me with it."

Amy gasped. He couldn't look at her. He couldn't bear to see the justice in her eyes that he got what he deserved.

"The entire time they called me so many names. I was sick, perverted, a freak and the devil. I didn't deserve to live or love; I would ruin everything. What I wanted wasn't sex, it was bestiality and degrading to woman, I deserved to rot in hell. I eventually blacked out. Matthew told me he found me and took me to the hospital. My skin was so badly marred that I was told I would be scarred for life. I vowed from that day I would take control. I would never put myself in that situation again. That is what I have done. I covered my back with the Angel to remind myself of that vow. Then I met you." He went silent. All he could hear in the room was Amy's small sobs. He still couldn't look at her.

"You...you...meant me?" She struggled to get her words out.

"Yes--and I lost control again." He finally looked up at her, and she had tears streaming down her face. "I don't want to lose you, Amy, please. I will try to be good. I will get counselling. I will do anything that it takes so that I don't make you hate me. I am sorry. I made you do things I shouldn't have. Please, please don't hate me. I don't want to be that person. I want to be the boyfriend that you need."

Amy turned away and let out an anguished cry. He had lost her. He knew it. She walked over to the table and picked up a scarf she had placed on it earlier. She came back to the bed.

"Stand up, James." Her words were barely distinguishable.

"What are you going to do?"

"You say you love me? Do you trust me?"

"Amy?"

"Do you?"

"Yes."

She shut her eyes and he watched as she took a deep breath.

"I am going to blindfold you."

"What?" Blindfold? She was going to teach him a lesson

as well. She was going to show him what a disgusting monster he was.

"Trust me." She came close to his face and whispered. He moved the sheet from over him and stood. He was still naked and extremely vulnerable before her. She tied the scarf around his face so he could not see. Maybe she was going to leave him like this and walk out on him. He may have just seen her for the last time.

She came close to his ear again and rested a hand on his chest, his heart was thumping so rapidly.

"James, you are not a freak, you are not the devil, you are none of those things. What you wanted is natural. Between two consenting adults, it is perfect and I enjoy everything that you do to me. Your ex-girlfriend wanted something different. What her brothers did to you was assault and it was wrong." She put a finger over his mouth as he went to correct her. "No. You have spoken and now I will. James. You are blindfolded before me. I am going to touch you wherever I want. You won't stop me. However, if at any point you really wish me to cease you will say Lanzarote. Do you understand?"

He nodded.

"James, I need you to say yes."

"Yes, Amy. I understand." He couldn't quite take in what she was saying to him just yet. It was confusing. It was not what he expected to hear from her. She should be angry; she should hate it. Yet here she was telling him what he wanted was natural.

"These scars," She was behind him now. "to you, show you to be nothing but vile and dirty. I am going to give them new meaning. I am going to show you that you are everything to me, that I love you and we will try new things together that are not sinful. They're right. They're right because we are in love and we consent." She kissed the centre of his back where he knew the heaviest of his scars were. The angel's sad face covered them. He groaned. She kissed him again. He felt his cock beginning to rise. His back was burning. Every time she pressed her lips against a part of it, it sent shivers throughout his body. She repeated the process again. Her delicate fingers traced what he knew were the outline of the scars hidden beneath the fanciful artwork. His thick cock was jutting rigidly out by the time she had finished. He was ready to explode.

"Amy."

"No talking, James. We are a partnership. No secrets, no lies. We are equals. If we don't agree or like something we use the word Lanzarote."

She stopped talking and he couldn't hear her moving. He was trying to listen out for where she was when her lips wrapped around his cock.

He moaned long and loud. She was sucking him hard, her tongue twisting around his shaft as she savoured every inch of him. He wouldn't last long. He was listening to her. They were both consenting in this. He wasn't hurting her or pushing her away. She wanted the crazy stuff as much as he did. She was enjoying it. That is why he lost his control with her. That is why she frustrated him, in equal parts to him loving her. He groaned again as he felt her swallow him deep. He was hitting the back of her mouth. He wanted to rip the blindfold off so he could watch her but he needed to come like this. The scars on his back were no longer stinging painfully. They were vibrating. They were pulsating waves of pleasure into his balls and as he felt the fires surging through his body; he called out her name as he came into her mouth. His legs threatened to give way and she helped him to sit back on the bed, she then removed the blindfold and was kneeling before him. Her hands rested on his toned thighs as his exhausted cock settled.

"James, I love you. I am not your ex-girlfriend. I don't want just vanilla sex with you. You want to blindfold me, whip me, use toys, fuck me in any position you want, I consent. I consent because it isn't wrong. It is something we are agreeing upon together. I may not say yes to everything, and equally there may be things I want to do to you that you don't. But we make this decision together, we discuss it, and we have a relationship of equals." He drew her up into his arms.

"You really don't hate me?"

"No, James. I can't live without you. I will be at your side forever."

He moved a strand of hair that had flipped over eyes and then wiped away the tears.

"I thought I was wrong for so many years. I never let anyone have control. God I must have annoyed Matthew and my mother."

Amy laughed.

"I don't expect you to change overnight. I think I would miss it actually. Shows you care."

"Equals."

"Equals."

Amy looked at the clock.

"You do realise we have to be up in three hours for the buffet breakfast."

He pulled her back into bed with him.

"I would rather have you for breakfast. If I am not a freak, I have a lot of things I want to try with you. I think I may have to send Matthew out to buy a copy of the Kama Sutra tomorrow."

CHAPTER TWENTY

Amy

Amy ran the brush through her hair and scooped it up into a ponytail. There wasn't any time to shower nor to wash the hairspray out of her hair from the previous night. She took her foundation and tried to disguise the bags that had appeared under her eyes. James was frantically running around trying to get his clothes on.

"Are you ready?" His voice was tense.

She gave herself a spray of her favourite Marc Jacobs perfume.

"Yes."

"Come on then."

They opened their bedroom door and Matthew and Sonia stood there immaculately ready, as if they had had the regulation eight hours sleep. Amy just wanted to go back to bed. She looked and felt a mess.

"I know. We are late." James held his hands up apologetically. "We had a lot to talk about."

Matthew scowled at James.

"Raji has been calling every five minutes. I told him to start without you."

"Thank you. Let's go."

James took Amy's hand, and they almost ran to the lift.

"Everything alright boss?" She heard Matthew try to whisper to James.

"It's perfect. I have a few things I want you to fetch for me later if you can find them."

Amy tried not to gulp too loudly; she knew he was referring to the newfound sexual freedom that she had given James and his urgency to explore it.

The breakfast buffet was already in full swing when they

arrived. Amy took her seat but James was immediately dragged off to engage in conversation with those that he hasn't managed to speak to the previous evening. Most people were helping themselves to the breakfast. It was a mixture of cereals, cheeses, hams, fruits, yoghurts and of course all the traditional British fry up ingredients. Amy wasn't really hungry so just asked Sonia if she would fetch her some fruit and a poached egg on toast. Her bodyguard had a look of worry on her face. Amy knew Sonia could see that she wasn't just physically exhausted but mentally as well.

"Are you alright, Amy? If you want to talk, you know I am a good listener."

"Thank you, Sonia." Amy hadn't wanted Sonia as her bodyguard, she felt she would impact on her freedom. She had often been harsh and not even spoken to her. However, during the trip they had spent a lot of time together and she had eventually told her to call her Amy, as Matthew did. Amy actually counted her as a friend. "Do you know everything?"

"Matthew asked permission from James to inform me of all the details." Amy noticed her clench her fist in anger. "What they did to him was wrong. He didn't deserve that."

"No. Not at all."

"I am glad he told you and that you stayed with him."

"He never did anything to make me want to leave him, Sonia. What he wants is natural to me. I just have to help him realise it as well." Amy blushed, "I am sorry, you probably don't really need to hear of my sexual preferences. It won't assist you in guarding me."

She took Amy's cup, "The more I know about you Amy, the better I can protect you. Please don't ever fear telling me anything." Sonia smiled and went off to find her breakfast.

Amy looked around the room for James, who was animatedly chatting with an elderly American couple. Amy couldn't believe how relaxed he looked. Last night his shoulders had been hunched up and his face was full of tension but despite only about two hours sleep he looked free from all the cares in the world. Amy was still struggling to get her head around how someone could've made him feel so dirty for a natural urge to want to explore his girlfriend's body. She wanted to explore his, to find out what he liked and what he didn't. She wondered if the ex-girlfriend had been as controlling in their lives out of the bedroom as well. Would he have been allowed to kiss her apart from a peck on the lips? What about holding hands in public? She could see why James was so controlling with her. After what happened he had closed down, he had not allowed himself to think about anything that he didn't prescribe himself.

The breakfast passed peacefully and when Amy saw that James wasn't actually going to be allowed to sit down and eat she had a coffee sent to him and a load of pastries taken to their bedroom. She returned to the bedroom without him, despite assurances he wouldn't be more than a few moments behind her and took a shower. The warm water cascaded off her aching muscles as she shut her eyes and allowed herself to really dream of a future with James. They hadn't known each other long but to Amy, it felt as though he was a part of her now. To not be in his arms would kill her. It must have been another hour before he appeared. He was chatting animatedly with Matthew as Sonia and Amy sat in the chairs watching a Bollywood film.

"They wanted to leave around one. How long is the flight?"

"A little under an hour I think."

"Alright. I want you to book us into one of the cabins for the night. Raji can see to the guests tonight. I am not the manager, merely the owner. And if I don't get some sleep this evening I am liable to collapse."

"You want me to have Miss Amy flown back here so you can sleep."

James glared and then thumped Matthew on the back.

"Miss Amy will do as she is told. Especially after I have

exhausted her."

"You want to bet on that James?" She butted into their conversation, and Sonia laughed. "Where are we going now?"

"A few of the guests want to take advantage of a package we can put together for them. It flies them down to Kabini Nature Reserve for a visit. Sorry beautiful, but we have to join them."

"I wondered why the hotel had the helipad. What do I need to wear?"

"Shorts and a t-shirt will be good. It will be hot down there."

She looked at the clock. It was already close to midday. "I will pack us an overnight back. You go shower and shave. Make sure you eat something as well."

"I will do." Matthew nudged him, "Oh, yes. I need you to sign this as well. It is just some papers for the landing cards at the Maldives."

Amy picked up a pen, signed and handed them back to James. She couldn't be bothered to read them. She trusted James. "I am sorry, Amy. I had hoped we could just spend some time together."

"James, this means the world to you. I am fine. Relax and go with it. Stop worrying. Besides a nature safari sounds good."

"You won't say that when you see the tour vehicles."

James was right. As Amy entered the bus that had opened windows and looked like it might not make the tour she suddenly felt a little nervous.

"What animals are we likely to see?"

"It will be mainly elephants, antelope and monkeys but there have been tigers, crocodiles and leopards before."

"You sure it is safe?" She looked at thc window.

"Hold me tight, just so you don't bounce out?"

"What?" He laughed and she punched him in the chest. "Don't tease me like that."

The tour was breath-taking, to see the animals in their

natural habitats especially the elephants was just fantastic. They were happy and relaxed. Amy noticed lots of little tree stumps on the plains. She queried the guide and was told that during monsoon weather, the plains flooded due to the amount of rain and thus the trees didn't grow. She couldn't imagine how much rain could flood somewhere, and she lived in England where it never seemed to stop raining. As they were heading back to the helicopter there was suddenly a lot of commotion between the driver and the guide. The bus halted abruptly. Amy looked to her right and there, striding out of the bushes, not more than about ten metres from them, was a leopard. It was magnificent. It seemed to be posing for them. Its sleek spotty coat was beautiful in design, the way its paws padded along the ground showed off its powerful feline abilities. James got out his phone and began to snap pictures as he spoke. "This is unique. I never saw a leopard before."

The whole bus hushed and just watched the big cat as it walked past the bus and then ran into the bushes on the other side. Amy reached up to him and kissed him.

"Thank you for bringing me here."

"Thank you for coming here with me."

They returned to the helicopter and waved their guests off before they got into a nearby Jeep. Matthew and Sonia stayed with them of course. Amy wondered if they ever got bored just following them around; mind you, the job did have some perks.

The vehicle bounced its way along the unmade roads towards holiday cabins on the outskirts of the reserve. The farmers were in the fields tending to the crops, they still used cows to pull things like ploughs. She didn't see a single tractor. Out here, unlike the city, it was like time stood still and everyone still lived life like in the olden days. Except for the satellite television dishes on all the houses, of course. The cabins they were staying in were old-fashioned wooden ones, except with modern conveniences. She knew what James liked by now, and so she wasn't surprised. It was dusk by the time they arrived and as they walked into their cabin, a romantic dinner for two had been laid out on the veranda, next to a hot tub.

A waiter appeared and began placing dishes on hot plates. James tipped him and he left them alone.

"Dinner, Miss Jones?"

"Why thank you, Mr North."

He pulled her chair out for her and she took a seat. The meal was again a traditionally Indian affair but Amy didn't mind. She had gotten very used to it and was really enjoying the variety. What she did particularly like though were the sweets that were placed out for dessert. They were made of marzipan and covered in gold and silver leaf. She could've eaten far too many of them, but she also fancied sometime in the hot tub.

"I am going for a soak in the hot tub. Ease the aching muscles from the dancing last night and the bouncing around in the tour bus."

"Did you bring your bikini? Do you want me to fetch it?"

"Damn it." Amy sighed and rolled her head. "You didn't tell me I needed it, so I didn't bring one." She pulled her t-shirt over her head and dropped it to the floor with her shorts. "I could just go in in my bra and knickers, what do you think?"

James sat back in his chair and brought his leg up over the arm and pretended to be deep in thought. "Well you could, but personally, I have heard stories of the chlorine in these things ruining clothes. I think you need to take them off completely."

"Oh yes. I wouldn't want to damage such beautiful underwear." Amy stepped into the candlelight so that she knew James could see her, and teasingly lowered the straps of her bra. She kept her eyes on him the entire time. She unhooked the bra and let her breasts free. She went to lower her knickers but James was upon her. He took hold of the fabric and tore them from her body. "So much for not getting them damaged."

"I will buy you new ones." his voiced rumbled through her body with its gravelly tones of lust. He dropped his shorts and pants and then pulled his t-shirt over his head.

"James." Amy reached out and touched his hand. "This is normal. I want to do it."

"I know. If you didn't, then you would say Lanzarote to me. And we would discuss it."

She nodded at him, she felt so happy as he guided her into the tub and pulled her onto his lap. She slid down on his already hard cock and he reached over and turned the jets on. At first, they didn't move. They just enjoyed being rocked by the current of the waves, Amy stared into James eyes, her forehead resting on his. This was intimate and intense.

"James, I am past the seven days that we needed to be careful. If you want. You can come inside me without a condom on?"

'Do you want that?"

"Yes."

"Then I want it too."

James placed his hands on her hips and began to guide her movements up and down his shaft. She let him take the control, he needed this, she just became lost in the feeling of his thick cock, free from any barriers, thrusting within her, he felt closer and deeper. She felt more connected to him than she had ever done. James increased the pace and she bobbed up and down in the water. Her breasts were just resting on the surface as she went down. As he pushed her up, his teeth sank into one, and Amy cried out. Shivers ran through her body. She could feel her orgasm building, but she wanted their first time skin on skin to be special. They needed to come together. She wanted him to feel every muscle of her private havens milking his cock for everything that he could give her. She wanted to drink it all inside her. Too much tension had existed between them and this moment was about freeing it all.

"James, can we come together?" Her heart was beating

rapidly and she was beginning to feel the pressure in her thighs as she now helped James with their movement.

"Amy, that is the only way I ever want to come again. Whenever you are ready. I will be there right with you, beautiful." he looked down to where their movements were becoming so frantic between them that the water was fountaining over the sides of the tub.

Amy leant forward and kissed his lips. What had started as tender lovemaking was now inflamed passion. The kiss was bruising in its urgency, and their bodies were driving together. Amy flung her head back as the orgasm came upon her vigorously and fast, she cried out and shuddered as she felt James' cum flow within her. Their essences combined as she came back to his lips and, neither of them moving now, just stayed there. All around them came the sounds of nature, the calls of the elephants over in the reserve and the crickets as they sang their evening songs.

CHAPTER TWENTY-ONE

James

"Come on. Stop being a wimp."

"But what if something bites my toes? Do they have teeth?"

"Amy, nothing will eat your toes. They may suck on them but they won't eat them."

"That doesn't sound much better. Argh. I can see fish swimming."

"That is usually what fish do, beautiful."

"But they will touch me. They will be slimy."

"They won't come anywhere near you. They're more scared of you than you are of them."

"I don't want to touch the bottom. You have to hold me the entire time so that I don't have to put my feet down. There may be crabs and they will bite my toes."

"I will hold you every single minute, Amy. Trust, remember?"

"Why did I agree to this?"

"Because you are the best girlfriend in the world."

"No, because you had me tied to the bed, blindfolded and were sucking my clit so hard I was screaming."

"Exactly, the best girlfriend in the world."

"James North, I am never letting you between my thighs again."

"Yeah right. I give you a day on that. Now get in the water, Amy."

James steadied himself as Amy finally dived into the water and clung to him like a limpet.

"Something touched my backside."

"That is me."

"Don't you even think of trying to get me horny, James."

"It was the furthest thing from my mind, Amy."

They had been in the Maldives for almost a week now and this was the first time they had actually ventured out of the bedroom. Amy had failed in a task the previous night, and this was her punishment. James had found out that she had never been snorkelling before as she was terrified of swimming with fish. He wasn't going to let her miss out on such a fantastic experience so when she had come, twice, without his permission, he had had Matthew book the excursion at once.

"James, please. They're going to touch me."

"Amy, relax. They're fish. Why don't you put your head under the water and have a look?" She shook her head rapidly. "Amy. I am going to put your mask down and put the breathing part in your mouth. Relax. I am protecting you." He pulled the mask over her eyes and before he could put the breathing tube in her mouth she spoke,

"James, if so much as one little fish touches me, you are having no sex for a month."

"Alright, Amy. If one fish touches you, then I will satisfy myself for a month."

" That is not what I meant."

"I know." He shoved the breathing part of the snorkel into her mouth before she could answer him. All he could hear was mumbled words. He was sure they involved numerous swear words. "Right, just put your head under the water. See what you can see. Remember to breathe normally but through your mouth." He could see that she was absolutely terrified but she did as he asked. Her head must have been under for at least two or three minutes before she came up gasping for breath. She spat the piece from her mouth,

"I saw an angelfish. It swam so near to me. It was so colourful. I want to go under again. But don't let me go."

"I won't."

Amy disappeared back under the water and eventually relaxed. James held her the entire time, and whenever a fish came too close she jumped up into his arms a little further. He couldn't believe that he was here, in the middle of the Indian Ocean with such an astounding woman. He had been such an idiot to believe what his ex-girlfriend and her family had called him. What they did together was natural. He could only put it down to the foolishness of youth that he had been sucked into what they made him believe. He hadn't relinquished all of his controlling nature just yet, though. He still expected high standards, and where Amy was concerned she was to be treated like a Princess at all time. She was his and he would make sure of that. He had the money so why not.

He had a surprise for her tonight. He was nervous about it, as she didn't want him to keep secrets that concerned them together but this had to be kept a secret. She would understand. Wouldn't she? God, he hoped so.

When they arrived back at shore, Sonia fell ill and Amy became very upset. Matthew was left to deal with Sonia, while James took Amy back out into the sunshine. Amy agreed that James could connect to his laptop and answer a couple of emails while she picked up a romance novel and began reading. He wondered if the romance was on a par with theirs. Amy laughed and told him theirs was better, maybe she should write about it, that would shock the press. He turned back to his emails happily and pictured the expression on the faces of the likes of Miss Sally Bridgewater. The afternoon passed far too quickly.

James sent Amy up to the villa to dress for dinner whilst he made the final few arrangements with Matthew and checked on Sonia who was feeling much better. He wanted everything to be perfect. When he entered the villa, he was delighted to find Amy naked and freshly showered. Dinner plans went out of the window for a few moments while Amy was given a little reward for her bravery in the water. James left her basking in the afterglow of her orgasm while he showered and changed into a pair of casual linen trousers and a shirt. When ready, he checked on Amy and found she was dressed in the white skater dress that she had worn the first time they met in Lanzarote. James had thought that most of her clothes hadn't survived her uncle's destruction of the flat but he was certainly glad this one did.

"You ready?"

"Yes. Are we going far?"

"No, not far at all." James picked up the blindfold from the table and handed it to her. "I want you to put this on, please."

"Oh no. The last time I wore that, I ended up swimming with fishes."

"No punishment, this time, Amy." James swallowed. "I have a surprise for you?"

"A surprise?" He could sense the nervousness in her voice.

"Are you upset?"

Amy came up to him. Pulled his shirt from his trousers, she went round his back and ran her hand over his tattoos. He moaned as sparks of pleasure coursed through his body. His tattoos no longer meant pain, they said happiness. She came back around to face him, took the blindfold, and put it over her eyes.

"I am ready."

James held her hand and lead her down to the beach. He was certain that he had butterflies in his stomach. Nothing had ever meant so much to him. When they got to the shore, he kept her a little distance while Matthew and Sonia lit the candles that they had placed out on the beach. The massive picnic hamper stood next to the blanket and cushions that had been laid out on the beach. Eventually, Matthew and Sonia left and James lifted the blindfold from Amy's eyes. The sun was just setting and the moment was perfcct. James took a seat on the blanket and Amy nestled into his arms and they watched the sunset together. James wasn't normally soppy but it was probably the most romantic moment of his life. He opened the hamper and gave Amy some strawberries and he popped the cork on a bottle of the finest champagne. He handed her a glass and they chinked to happiness and love. James was about to speak when Amy started up a conversation.

"James, I have decided something while I have been here. I want to sell my flat, and use the money to rent a dance studio and teach dance. I have experience, though no real teaching qualifications. I am sure I can find a qualified teacher to help me out. What do you think?"

"What about your writing?"

"I will still be able to do that. It won't be full time. My writing is novels. It isn't journalism or anything like that. As long as I manage a daily quota, I will be alright."

"You know that you don't need to work right? I can provide for you and I want to."

"I know. And that is why I want to set the dance studio up. It doesn't have to be for money. It can be for fun and for teaching others to do something that I love. It would be nice if it made some money, but I am not business-minded at all. I will leave that to you."

"You want me to help you?"

"Not with money, but maybe with things such as finding the studio."

"It would make more financial sense to keep the apartment in Kennington and use the rent and the money you have saved so far for deposit and rent payments. Maybe I could invest a little to make up any shortfall you may have. I would expect a return on my investment, though." He grinned at her. Amy didn't reply to him; he could see she was working a response out in her head. "I would be a silent partner, Amy. I can draw up an official loan contract for the money and expect regular returns when you can afford it and even payment for my business' services to you."

"At a commercial rate?"

"At a rate that we sit down and discuss together and agree on."

"I don't know. Wouldn't it just be easier to get rid of the flat?"

"I would prefer you to keep it for a safety net."

"In case we break up?"

"No, because that won't be happening. In case you need it in an emergency for any reason."

She smiled.

"Alright, we will work out a deal when we are back in England. No wonder you are so successful Mr North; you drive a hard bargain."

"It is what I am known for, Amy."

"Can we toast it with a little more of this champagne?"

"I hope that you are not going to get drunk on me, Amy. This isn't the only romantic surprise I have for you tonight."

"Oh yes? What else?"

"You will have to wait a bit."

"Tease."

"I think after this week Amy; you have learnt that if I want to tease you I can. And I will make you scream my name while doing it."

"I love it when you talk all masterful."

"I love it when you submit. Food?"

"Only if you eat it from my stomach."

"Amy."

"Spoilsport."

He handed her a plate of food and they sat watching the rest of the sunset while eating. When the sun had finally disappeared beneath the ocean, it was time. He got to his feet and tried to disguise the fact he was shaking.

"Amy."

"Hmm." She sleepily replied as she laid back against the cushions.

"Amy. Look at me."

She instantly snapped awake and scrambled up onto her knees in front of him. He loved the way she reacted to him. He didn't even need to try to be masterful with her, she just responded.

"Sorry, is it time for another romantic surprise?"

"It is." James' palms were sweating; he had never been so

nervous. He could stand up in front of a room full of people but this one simple thing to his girlfriend and he was a quivering mess. He had had a whole speech prepared but his mind was jelly. He could not remember a thing, even his name it seemed.

"James, what is it? What is wrong."

Amy tried to get up but he got down on one knee in front of her. He pulled a little box from out of his pocket. The sea lapped around them onto the white gold sand. The candles flickered in the moonlight, and a thousand stars shone down on them expectantly.

"Amy, I know that in the grand scheme of things we have not known each other very long, but I am confident about this. I am more certain than I have ever been about anything in my life. I love you, and I want to share the rest of my life with you." He cleared his throat. "Will you marry me?" James opened the little box he had before him. Inside was a platinum ring with a princess cut diamond. He had had the ring flown in from Dubai and it had been specially made to his specifications. He held his breath as he waited for Amy to answer.

He knew what was in his heart. He never wanted to even look at another woman. From the moment he had met her in Lanzarote he had been enthralled with her. She had gotten under his skin and helped him recover from his past. Yes, he was still demanding but she understood him and could temper that with her playfulness. Had he made a big mistake? Had he ruined everything?

"James." Here was the put-down. He could hear it in her voice.

"It is ok, Amy. I am sorry. I shouldn't have asked. It is too soon, right? I should have told you. I shouldn't have just got the ring. I am taking control again and not telling you things. I will put it away and send it back." He got to his feet and shut the box.

"James North, will you stop over-analysing things and let me answer. Open that box up and come and put that ring on my finger." She held her hand out.

"What?"

"James, I love you. Even if you are an idiot sometimes. Yes, I will marry you. I don't ever want to be apart from you. I can't take a breath when I am." She was crying now. His eyes were watering as well. Must have sand in them. He took her left hand and slid the ring on. He could've spent more money on a ring for her but she had delicate hands and anything ostentatious would have looked awful. He had judged it just right.

"Perfect."

"It is." She held her hand up and looked at the ring. "Oh my God. I will be your wife."

"That is generally what happens when two people get married, Amy."

"Can we celebrate our engagement?"

"What do you have in mind?" She reached down to his trousers. He stopped her. "Alas beautiful, not really the best thing to be doing in the open in this country. However, let's go back to the bedroom. I have one more surprise for you."

CHAPTER TWENTY-TWO

Amy

James led Amy into the bedroom. They had left everything on the beach but she knew Matthew would dutifully arrange for it to be cleared up. She wondered what they would ever do if Matthew left them. They would probably never get anything done and get arrested for doing something wrong. He was only a couple of years older than James, but he was almost like big brother.

Amy looked down at her hand and the glistening gem on her ring finger. She had had no idea that James was going to propose to her, let alone present her with the most beautiful ring she had ever seen. It had caught her completely by surprise. She had had to take a few minutes to repeat his words in her head until she fully understood what he was saying. When she realised, she had no hesitation in saying yes. She loved James; she wanted to be his wife more than anything in the world.

When her parents had died she had thought her life was over, she had relied on them for so much love and support and all of a sudden she was alone. Yes, she had had her uncle but now that she looked back, she had always seemed an inconvenience to him. Probably why he didn't care less about the fact she could've been raped. She was glad he was out of her life and hoped that she never had to see him again. She had a new life; she would be Mrs North. She would look after the man to whom she was devoted but she would still have time to herself to pursue her dancing interests and writing. In Matthew and Sonia, she had friends and close ones at that. They had all eaten together one night on the trip as a thank you from James for all their hard work and support. The evening had been so joyous and full of laughter that she was certain by the end they would all ache the next morning from collapsing in fits of giggles. Amy was sure something was going on between Matthew and Sonia as well. The atmosphere between them had changed. She had mentioned it to James, who laughed and said he thought Matthew was celibate. He had never even so much as looked at a girl since he had been with him.

And she had Miranda, who had become like a surrogate mother to Amy. She was so caring and reminded Amy of how much she missed her own mother. She hoped Miranda would be pleased to hear of the engagement. She was a little nervous about telling her.

"Did your mother know you were planning to propose?"

James had gone to the drawer when they entered the room that Amy knew he kept some of the 'provisions' that Matthew had got for him in India. He turned around and looked at her.

"Way to ruin the thoughts in my head, Amy. I really don't need to be thinking about my mother at the moment."

"Sorry. I just wondered. Would she be worried that we haven't been together long?"

"She adores you as much as I do Amy. Yes, I did tell her that I was going to propose. I told her what happened after I told you everything about me. She is over the moon for us and said that if I do anything to chase you away, she will disown me."

"I like your mother. She is a sensible lady."

"I like her, too, but right now, I would rather you remove all of your clothes and we banish any more thoughts of my mother from our minds. It is not conducive to what I have planned." He looked down at his groin.

Amy, lowered her dress to the floor as the sides of her mouth curled up in amusement. Something about just even getting naked before James and seeing the way he looked at her body had her quivering with anticipation.

"What do you plan on doing to me tonight?" She sauntered up to him. As in Lanzarote, she had not worn a bra with the dress, she didn't need to, so all that she had on was her knickers. He pulled some lubricating gel out of the drawer and placed it on the counter top. He then pulled out a vibrator as thick as he was. It pulsated at such a rapid speed that just one touch against her clit the other night had almost had her screaming out in orgasm.

"Amy. Normally I would ask that you don't question me on what I am going to do to you. I want you to feel the heightened sense of knowing that I will get you off hard but not how I will do it." He tore her knickers from her body and ran his hand over her sensitive mound. She was wet for him already. She didn't know why he needed the gel. She was always dripping for him with just one look. "But this is a big thing for us both. I own here; this is my pussy. It responses to any commands that I give it, even when here," — he pressed a kiss to her forehead— "is being stubborn."

James removed his hand from where he had been massaging her and Amy pouted in the loss of friction. He gave her a quick tap to her clit, which elicited a moan of shock and pleasure from Amy. He then traced his hand over her hip and around her back and down the crack of her backside. He stopped at the small puckered hole. "I want to explore here."

Amy heard him inhale a breath as he spoke and waited for her response. "I have never done that before. Have you?"

"Yes, Amy. Once with the lady I told you about."

He was honest to her. That meant a lot.

"She would have been used to it I suspect."

"I suspect as well. I have been preparing you all week to take me, though. You may not have realised, but every time I used a butt plug with you I used a bigger one. Amy, if you don't want to, please just say. I will do something different. We have a lifetime together to explore these things, when and if you feel ready."

"It is not that I don't, I like it when you play there. It

heightens my orgasms. I am scared though. I worry it will hurt. You aren't exactly small."

"We will take it slowly. See how you feel. You ask me to stop and I will."

"Alright. Let's try."

James dropped his clothes to the floor and lead Amy to the bed. He laid her down affectionately upon it and climbed beside her. Amy put her left hand on his face. The ring sparkled in the dim light of the room. A gift from her fiancé. The man who held her heart. They kissed, and the kiss turned more passionate as yet again they sought to feel every part of each other's bodies, Amy no longer worried about her hands caressing James's back. He allowed her to touch him freely, he even called out in pleasure when she ran a path over his scars. They no longer meant pain and suffering to him, they said love. Her love, a love she gave freely and with no constraints. Their bodies moved together as one as he entered her pussy and re-claimed that first as his own. His thrusts became animalistic and hard as she writhed underneath him. Then he slowed again, as she trembled on the precipice of orgasm. She cursed him as she always did but she knew that there was more and better to come. He pulled out of her and flipped her over and in one fluid movement plunged his rock solid cock deep into her pussy. She screamed out. She wanted him to move because in this position, he would rub against her g-spot every time that he did. He didn't, though. He reached over, took the lubricant, squeezed some of it against his hands, while she tried desperately to get some friction against where she needed him moving the most. He slapped her bottom and she called out in desperation again.

"James, please."

"Wait." His tone was masterful. He was at his dominating best at that very moment. She would do anything he wanted because she and her body were completely under his control. He was the only one that could give her the feelings that she craved. She hissed as she felt his finger test the pucker of her anus. Fuck. She wanted him there as well. She wanted him everywhere. He was already in her brain, her heart, her pussy. He teased his finger in slowly, as he did he started to move his cock within her. It felt painful for a mere second but after the pop which sucked him in, it felt so good. He ran his finger deeper and then gently pushed another in. She felt full. She felt complete.

"God I can feel my cock inside you. I can feel every time I move. Is it hurting?"

"No." She struggled to reply as she suppressed the orgasm bearing down on her like a stampede of wild horses.

"Come for me like this, Amy?"

She didn't need asking twice, Amy exploded around his cock. Shuddering and pulsating in an orgasm so fierce she could barely keep a sense of what was going on. As still stilled, James removed his fingers from within her but kept his cock inside her pussy. He didn't move. He just leant forward and held her until she got her breath back.

"Are you alright?"

"Yes. That was intense."

"Do you feel sore?"

"No."

He withdrew himself from within her pussy, covered himself with a condom and moved his cock to her arse.

"Can I try this Amy?"

"Yes." She didn't care if it hurt at first, she just wanted him inside of her. Anywhere. She needed to be joined with him. It was the only way she felt satisfied. James leant back on the bed and got the vibrator. He slid it inside her pussy, turned it on, and the fire ignited within her belly again. He took some of the lube and massaged it into her before pressing the head of his cock against her anus. He was so big it burnt as he pushed in, pausing to allow her sphincter to relax, then moving again, pausing again. Amy shut her eyes and tried to concentrate on the vibrator pulsating within her pussy, the pleasure that she got every time that it rubbed against her sweet spot inside her, but the burn came through. She didn't think she could do this. It was too much. But then the heat of delight hit. James was completely in her arse and he was grinding against the vibrator. She knew he was completely lost in the feeling. She could hear it in his breathing.

He withdrew from her. She instantly felt empty. He thrust back in and she squealed.

"Again." The word left her mouth before she was even able to fully register the feelings that were flooding her body. He pulled out and thrust into her again until he found a steady rhythm.

Their bodies were covered in sweat. This coupling between them was raw and untamed. It was new and they were learning. It was setting them both free from fear. Every time he thrust into her she felt herself on the verge of soaring. She was ready to fly, she had never felt so in love, she had never felt so free and so much pleasure. She was close. She could tell James was as well. The thrusting was getting quicker. James moved his hand to her clit and that was all Amy needed, she came in a furious explosion, and then she felt James coming inside her. Their bodies shuddered together. James withdrew and she collapsed down on the bed. He pulled her into his arms, holding her tight and stroking her damp locks from her forehead.

"Are you alright?"

"Yes, James, how do you know my body so well?"

"Because it was made for me. Just as I was for you."

He got up from the bed, disposed of the condom, fetched a cloth, and wiped Amy down. He then climbed into the bed beside her, and she snuggled into his arms.

"I need to sleep. I think you have just pushed me to the limit of what my body can handle"

"Oh no, you can handle a lot more, but for now I think I could do with some sleep as well."

"I don't think I want to go home tomorrow."

"I don't either, but we have to."

"Damn."

"Goodnight, Mrs North to be."
"Goodnight, Mr Jones to be."

CHAPTER TWENTY-THREE

James

James swept Amy into arms and carried her across the threshold of his mansion in Knightsbridge.

"You do realise that we are not married yet don't you?" Amy squirmed in his arms and tried to get him to put her down. He shrugged in reply.

"I know, just getting in practice for when we are. Besides, I know, it is quicker for me to get you to the bedroom if I don't let you walk."

"How do you work that one out?"

"You are a woman. You will want to show my mum the ring and then talk about the holiday and India. It will be at least 5 hours by the time I get you naked again."

"James you had me naked and in the mile-high club again not more than two hours ago."

"Yeah, but that was two hours ago."

She bashed his chest with her tiny fist, and he reluctantly put her down with a lamenting grumble. He wrapped his arms around her waist and affectionately kissed the top of her head.

"How you are going to survive a whole day at work is beyond me."

"You will be bringing me my lunch every day Miss Jones, that is how."

"Oh, yes? I thought that was what you had Matthew for?"

"I don't find him nearly as sexy as you. He likes to try and take the lead as well, he isn't a very good submissive."

The bodyguard grunted from behind him as he carried a heavy bag and dumped it on the floor.

"At least that is one duty I can stop performing for him then. I don't get paid enough to listen to that sort of moaning."

Amy laughed, and James just frowned at Matthew.

"You wish, Matthew." James looked around; he had expected his mother to greet them. "Mum?"

"I bet she has gone out to get the ingredients for your favourite meal. She told me when I text her earlier that she was going to cook it in celebration," Amy took her hand luggage from James as she spoke. "I will just put this in the bedroom, and then make us a cup of tea. I don't know about you lot, but I don't think I have had a decent cup of tea for two weeks now. You need to look at that for your hotel James." He smacked her bottom for her teasing.

"I will have you know I had the finest English teas imported. And this is in a country that is famous for making the stuff."

As Amy glided along to the bedroom, James watched the seductive sashay of her hips. She was his woman. They would be married soon and able to spend the rest of their lives happily together. He couldn't believe it. He needed to find a wedding planner for Amy straight away. He didn't want to wait for her to become Mrs North. He wondered if she would consent to going to Gretna Green at the weekend and marry there? His mother would kill him if he did. And so would his sister. She had been planning her wedding for ages, and she would have to be the first. He wanted to make sure Amy would never escape from him though. Not that he thought she actually would want to go anywhere despite how annoying he could be at times. James placed his hand luggage down on the floor and began heading for the kitchen to put the kettle on for Amy when he heard her scream. It was a bloodcurdling scream, one of sheer terror and panic. James turned quickly, and he and Matthew stormed for the bedroom. James almost skidded into Amy.

"The bed" She was sobbing. "He has her."

All the covers had been torn from their bed. Blood covered them, and a massive knife was embedded in the centre of their bed. He nodded to Matthew and he went to look at it. James edged closer, next to the knife was a fingernail that had been pulled off someone. That is where the blood came from. James swallowed back the feelings of compounding unease. The knife was stabbed through a picture of his mother, gagged and bound to a chair. There was a note. He looked to Matthew as he picked it up. Amy was still sobbing in his arms.

"What does it say?"

"If you want her back, and not a piece at a time, you will meet me and give me what I want. Come alone. My whore of a niece will tell you where."

James fought back the bile that was threatening to launch from his mouth with the thought that Amy's uncle had his mother and was hurting her. Why now? How did they get in here? This place was impenetrable. After Amy had come to live here, he had made sure of that with a thorough review of his security.

"We need to call the police?"

Amy lifted her head from his chest and spoke but still clung tightly to him.

"No." James' tone was unwavering. "No police." He nodded to Matthew, "Go fetch everything we need. I will meet you in the car in a few moments. Get Sonia in here now as well."

"James, you have to call the police. You can't go to him." Her big eyes stared up at him in panic. She thought he was crazy.

James picked the picture up, and his hand was shaking with fury. "Where is she, Amy?"

"James."

"Amy, where is my mother?" He shouted as his blood reached boiling point and she backed timidly away from him.

"Call the police, and I will tell them where she is. I am not telling you while you are in this frame of mind."

She turned away from him and refused to look at the picture anymore. He really didn't need her being stubborn right now. He needed to get to his mother and rip her fucking uncle's head off. He swung her back to face him. Probably a little too forcefully. His fingers dug into the delicate flesh of her arms.

"Amy, stop messing around with me. I don't have the time for this. He said you could tell me where he has my mother. Now tell me." James positioned his face mere inches from Amy's.

"James, I don't want you going to him. He will hurt you. Please. Please call the police." Amy dared to reach up and touch his heaving chest. He could see that she was absolutely terrified but he couldn't back down. His need to control had taken over him again and he just needed to be pointed in the right direction to go kill.

"Amy, your uncle took no qualms in killing his girlfriend. Sara, remember her. He is a fucking psychopath; he was going to allow me to rape you. His own flesh and blood. Amy, please, that man has my mother. I will be okay. You have to trust me alright. Please, Amy, tell me where he is, tell me where he has her?"

He held the picture up to her face. Defeat washed over her face and she bowed her head. "It is a room in the club, furthest from the stage, to the right. It is called the 'night' room. It is where he has the girls that do the darkest stuff. Please, James, if you are going, then I am coming with you. He wants me. For whatever reason, he wants me."

James cupped her chin. Amy was shaking, tears still streamed from her eyes. He needed to calm her down and reassure her before her left her alone. "He asked for me Amy, not you. I made him lose face by taking you away the way I did. He thought he would get ten thousand pounds, he got nothing. He will want money. I will give it to him, and this will all be over. You stay here and make that cup of tea. Mum will need it when I get her back."

"Is that what Matthew has gone to get? Money?"

"Yes, Amy. Matthew is getting him money. More than I promised him before."

Sonia coughed at the door. James kept his eyes focused on Amy, still trying to calm her down.

"Matthew is ready in the car, sir."

"You stay here, Amy. I will be okay. Sonia will be with you the entire time. I will phone you as soon as I have my Mother."

He saw Amy look to the door behind him, and her eyes widened with shock. She had seen the gun that Sonia was holding for him. Sonia quickly tried to hide it, but it was too late.

"You are taking a gun." She whacked him in the chest and pushed him away.

"Amy, calm down. It is for protection."

"You are not going to give him money, are you? You are going to kill him." She ran her fingers through her hair and pulled on the ends.

"If he doesn't see sense, yes."

She pushed past James and began to head for the telephone on the bedside table. James didn't have time to think. He ripped it from the wall.

"No police, Amy. This is personal, and I will deal with it my own way."

"James, you are scaring me." Amy had flattened herself again the wall, her eyes were bewildered as she tried to take everything in. Mere moments again they were returned from a romantic break full of love and excitement for their engagement but now; now the world was falling apart around them.

"Amy, you think I haven't done something like this before? What do you think happened to the brothers? I made sure they wouldn't hurt anyone else with their misguided preaching. Why do you think I have an ex-spy as my personal protection?"

"You killed them?"

"No. I have never killed anyone. But I have had to take people to task before. Matthew has trained me to be strong and protect myself. I have to go. We will talk more later.

My family is my responsibility, and I won't let anyone hurt them and get away with it." He stroked her cheek and she leaned into his caress.

"You are not going anywhere without me."

"I am sorry, Amy." Her face registered to late what he was about to do, and he pushed her into the bedroom, slamming the door shut behind him. Sonia handed him a key, and he locked the door. "I am so sorry Amy."

His head rested against the door as her tiny fist pounded it from inside. He shut his eyes, composed himself, and turned to Sonia. "Stay with her. Don't let her out for any reason until I get back. If you do, you will never work again in this country, even if you are fucking Matthew. Do you understand me?"

Sonia nodded. James took the gun from her and placed it into his jeans and headed down to the garage to find Matthew. He was certain he could still hear Amy's screams when he reached the basement. He hoped she would forgive him for this.

CHAPTER TWENTY-FOUR

Amy

Amy's hand hurt from thumping the heavy oak door. She fell to the floor, wiped the tears from her eyes and sat there in disbelief. James had lost it and had locked her in their bedroom. He was racing off to do god knows what and maybe even get himself killed. She had to stop him. He didn't know her uncle. Yes, she had thought butter wouldn't melt in his mouth once, but she had also seen the dark side to him and the damage that his hired thugs could do, like when a punter got out of hand at the club and left with broken limbs. They didn't have a brain cell between them. She had to get to James.

"Sonia, you have to let me out. Please." Amy got to her feet and calmed her voice as she spoke through the door.

"I am sorry, Amy. You know I can't do that." Sonia's voice was tempered as her bodyguard was also reeling from the rather unexpected welcome home.

"Sonia, James is in trouble. He doesn't know what he is headed into to. Please, Sonia. Matthew will be in danger too. Sonia, I have seen the way you look at him. I know that look. I wear it on my face all the time. Please, Sonia, I love James so much if anything happened to him I wouldn't survive. Do you feel that way about Matthew?"

"Amy, Matthew will be level-headed the whole time. He will know what he is doing. I want to let you out but I can't. Take a seat and wait. It won't be long and we will hear something. I am sure of that."

"Wait for the police to come and tell me that my fiancé is dead? Not going to happen. I will get myself out, even if I have to tie sheets together and climb out of the bedroom window."

Amy yelled out in frustration and smashed her fist into the door again. She saw her bag on the floor. Her mobile was in it. She could phone the police. She scrambled across the room and began to frantically pull all the belongings out. Where was it? Damn it. When she finally found it, she hugged it to her chest and almost let out a squeal of jubilation. Until she turned the screen over to face her.

"No, No, No."

It was out of battery.

"Amy what are you doing in there?"

Sonia's voice came through the door.

"Trying to sort this mess out as you won't help me."

"Amy, whatever you are doing stop it. Amy, please? Just wait. "

"Open the door and stop me then."

Amy got to her feet and went to besides James' bed. He kept a spare iPhone charger plugged into the wall there. She quickly plugged the phone in and waited, not very patiently for it to charge.

"Come on you damn thing. Work."

How long had James been gone? Ten? Fifteen minutes? He would be there soon. She didn't have much time.

Hurry up, hurry up.

"Amy. Please, just be patient." Sonia's voice was desperate now.

"Patient? Like fuck, Sonia. Do you know what my uncle is capable of? He is the reason you are employed to protect me."

"Amy. Lock yourself in the bathroom" Sonia screamed her name and advice this time. A thud came from the other side of the door.

"Sonia?" Amy stepped towards the door. No sound came from the other side.

"Sonia?" Amy shouted louder and ran to the door. The key turned, and it opened.

Sonia lay on the floor. Dead? Unconscious? Amy didn't know. She looked up and into the dead eyes of two of her uncle's thugs. Amy had to think quick. She couldn't get out of the bedroom; hiding in the bathroom wasn't an option.

The knife. Matthew had left it on the bed. She made a dash for it and grabbed it, just as one of the men caught her around the waist. She turned and slashed at his face. He screamed out in pain and let her go. Blood squirted from a gash that tore down his stubbled cheek.

"Stay away from me."

"Fucking bitch."

"You touch me, and I won't hesitate to use this knife as you can see."

"Amy, don't be so stupid. Your uncle just wants a little chat." The other man spoke as he strode confidently into the room, his hands were held high in supplication though.

"Where is James' mother? If you have hurt her--" She looked towards the fingernail on the bed.

"We only took one."

The man that didn't have blood pouring from his face lunged for her, but she slashed at his arm and managed to dash for the door. She wanted to check on Sonia, but she didn't have time; she had to get to the club. As she sped through the hallway she noticed the keys for the Audi on the side table. She grabbed them and headed down the stairs to the garage. Her heart was beating so fast she could hear it in her head. Footsteps echoed on the floor above. She stumbled on the stairs but managed to grab hold to the barrier to keep her upright. She tore into the garage and clicked the keys for the Audi. It opened and she jumped in and started the engine. She had never driven this thing. It had so many different buttons. She just wanted the button which allowed her to go. She found drive, pressed that and floored the accelerator just as the two thugs hurtled down into the garage. Amy clipped one of them as she sped past. His body flew off the bonnet and landed with a sickening crunch on the floor. She didn't have time to worry if she had killed him. The garage door was thankfully still open and she emerged onto the street above.

A car pulled in front of her. She had to slam on the brakes and whacked her head on the steering wheel. She tried to reverse but couldn't. She was trapped. The feeling of failure began to constrict her stomach. The door was flung open her uncle's head guard pulled her like a rag doll from the vehicle.

Leon was the only guard with half a brain. He was strong, devious, and liked to get his own way. There had been many a time in the club that Amy had seen him hit some of the girls if they'd done something wrong. He was also well known for taking pleasure from the girls, whether they wanted to or not.

"Miss Jones, can we stop with the feeble escape attempts now? If you want to see your lover alive again. I would come quietly."

Amy kicked him in the shin, but she couldn't get herself free. She was screaming, hoping someone would hear something and call the police if she could stall them for long enough.

She stilled immediately, however, when a gun was pointed at her head.

"Come on Leon, let me shoot the bitch."

"Boss wants her alive. We won't get our payoff if she is dead. I will let you play with her afterwards, though. She always did think she was better than the rest of us."

"I just heard the rumours that your dick was so small it wasn't worth worrying about."

He whacked his calloused hand hard across the face. She tasted blood in her mouth. He then pulled her face towards him and held her tight.

"I will show you just how much satisfaction I can give. Maybe a little display in front of your lover?" Amy spat in his face. Leon threw her at the other thug, whose face Amy had slashed. "Get her in the car. The neighbourhood watch 'round here will have called the police. We need to get out of here."

"What about Jase? She hit him with the car."

"Is he alive?"

"No idea."

"Let's hope he isn't. Now get her in the car."

Amy was thrown forward and into the car that she had crashed into. She just needed to relax, keep her calm, and use her brain. She knew her uncle better than anyone. He must have a weakness. What was it?

CHAPTER TWENTY-FIVE

James

"Are you sure about this, boss?" Matthew pulled the car up outside the club. "He isn't like anything you have faced before."

"He has my mother."

"He is also your fiancée's uncle. "

James gripped the dashboard tightly; his knuckles were white with fury. Matthew would do as he was asked, even if he felt James was going about it the wrong way.

James checked the gun, handed it to Matthew, and got out of the car. "Wait here. I will sound the alarm when I need you. Get my mother out first. I will get myself out."

"As you wish."

Matthew turned the engine off and waited, eagle-eyed, as instructed. James hated this bit. James hated it himself; his palms were sweating. They had only done this a couple of times together. James really hadn't lied to Amy when he said that he hadn't killed anyone. He hadn't, but Matthew had. On his say so.

After James had left the hospital, after the beating, he'd had Matthew follow the brothers. One night, they discovered them about to attack a gentleman outside of a gay club. They prevented the attack and dispensed their own justice on the brothers. Matthew had killed the older of the two. The other brother they had forced to leave the country for good, and he wouldn't walk properly again.

So this was nothing new to them, but it felt so much more personal. His mum was everything to him, she had supported him through so much. He wasn't about to let anything happen to her. Amy was his future and the thought that the man doing this was related to her made matters even worse. He knew that no matter what happened, Amy was going to end up hurt--better emotionally than physically.

He entered the club and was immediately frisked by a bodyguard, his phone was taken away, and he was led down the corridor to the back. The club was empty. James was shown into a dark room. Again, as Amy had said, knives, whips, and chains were on the wall. His mum was in the centre of it. He ran to her and checked her. She was crying, and her hand was covered in blood. Somebody would pay for this. She pulled away from him. She was blindfolded and had headphones over her ears--she didn't know it was him. He went to remove them, but a voice behind him spoke. "I wouldn't do that Mr North; she tends to scream a lot when you remove the blindfold. I wish I had taken her tongue instead of a nail. Mind you, it wasn't as bad when I was fucking her, pretending to be her loving boyfriend."

James slowly stood up, his fists clenched and he exhaled sharply to keep his composure. He spun to face Amy's uncle and three guards.

"So that is how you got in my house. Clever. Name your price, I will pay and then I can get home to my fiancée, and we can forget you ever existed. My driver is in my car; I will send him to get it."

"Oh no Mr North, this has gone so much deeper than that. You see, I found something out. Those papers I sent to you in India for Amy to sign? Well, They're worthless."

James swallowed hard. Something he thought was over and forgotten was coming back to haunt him.

"Worthless? They handed the club over to you, which is what you wanted. And Amy doesn't know that she even owned it in the first place."

"Yes, she can't sell the club. A stipulation of her father's will, not until she is twenty-five. And I am sure you can appreciate that I am not willing to wait that long."

"I will get my lawyers to look into it at once. Amy doesn't have to know about that. She thinks you are out of her life. She doesn't want you back."

"No. That isn't enough anymore. I have been messed around enough, and as it seems things are very serious between you and my niece. Why should I not profit from it? I want ten million."

"I don't have that money laying around." James raised an eyebrow in derision.

"I've researched your finances, and I know you can access your money at any time. I could however, take a down payment until you can get the rest to me. I will post one piece of your mother back to you each day until I get what I want. I am thinking a finger next. What do you say?"

"I won't be able to get that sort of money from here. Let me send my bodyguard in to stay with my mother, and I will go get the money."

Amy's uncle rubbed his head. "Micky. Remove Mrs North's finger. It seems Mr North is determined to play with us."

Micky moved towards James's mother with a knife in hand. James moved his hands together as if to plead, and pressed a button on his watch. That would give Matthew the alarm he needed to come in and finish this. James just needed a little time.

"No. Please. If I take that much money out of my accounts, it is designed to trigger alarms. I need to do it in person. I am not messing with you. I wouldn't risk my mother. Please." He kept his voice deliberately calm.

James moved forward to try and distract the guard that had the gun pointed at him. The guard put the gun down and went to grab James. James allowed himself to be restrained just as Matthew appeared, and in one quick shot, fired a bullet through Mickey's head. Matthew turned the gun on the guard beside Amy's uncle and shot him in the leg before he could get a clear aim at either James or his mum. James flipped the guard who held him in place over his shoulder and rammed him head first into the wall. He slumped to the ground. James grabbed the gun from the table as Matthew knocked the other guard out as well. Both James and Matthew turned the gun on Amy's uncle, ready to shoot. But something was wrong.

He didn't look scared. In fact, he still wore the confident smile on his face.

"Matthew, untie my mother and get her out of here."

Matthew nodded and removed the blindfold.

"Do you even know how to use that gun?" Stephen Jones was taunting James but he responded by cocking the pistol and pointed it squarely at Amy's uncle's forehead.

"I may be a simple businessman, but unfortunately, I have seen enough fuckers like you in my life to need to know how to protect myself."

"You ever killed any of them, though? Isn't that what he is for?" He raised his eyebrows towards Matthew.

"We shall see very shortly won't we?"

"We will. Because you won't be killing me here today. You will be giving me what I asked for."

"Are you an idiot?"

"No but it would seem you are. And a predictable one at that."

"What is that supposed to mean?"

Matthew appeared at James' side with his mother.

"Let's go, boss."

"Oh, I wouldn't." Amy's uncle laughed with a cackle. "Our party is just beginning. I would suggest you drop the guns." His eyes flicked towards the back of the room. Matthew turned his head whilst James kept his eyes boring into the evil before him. Matthew sighed and bent to put his gun on the ground and kicked it away.

"Boss, drop the weapon."

James spun around.

Amy stood before him, her hands cuffed behind her back, a bump on her head, and blood staining her mouth. Next to her stood a man who held her tightly, whispering in her ear so that Amy's face screwed up in revulsion. James didn't need to lip read to know what was being said, especially when the man licked Amy's face. Tears tumbled down her face. To the other side of her stood a man with a gun at her head. James pointed his own gun down and bent to lay it on the floor. It had all been a trap. His mother was a ruse to allow them to take the real prize. The woman he loved more than anything. He had vowed to protect her, but he had failed. He needed to get his head straight, but he couldn't. His need to control would destroy everything. It already had.

CHAPTER TWENTY-SIX

Amy

Amy recoiled as Leon licked her face. He had been touching her and insinuating all sort of lewd things all the way to the club. She wanted nothing more than to smack him in his tiny balls.

James put the gun down and stood with his hands up. The guard with the weapon at Amy's head gave his gun to Leon and stepped forward to collect the ones Matthew and James had placed on the ground. Her uncle's guards were rapidly dwindling, two lay unconscious on the floor, one lay dead from a bullet to his forehead, and the one that Amy had injured had disappeared for medical attention the second they had dropped Amy here. He probably also went back to collect his mate that she had run over. She tried to remember how many other guards were around. She thought this was it. The guard with the guns placed them on a table. At her uncle's command, he then strapped Matthew into a set of chains on the wall. They knew he was the one to watch. Miranda kept close to his side.

Amy looked at James, and she could see that he was lost again. She had seen that fear before. He was suffering. He had seen that Amy was hurt and shut himself down as he blamed himself for causing her pain. She needed to bring him back and the only way she could do that was by being the strong one as she had been in the past.

This was how their relationship worked. When one needed the other, they were always there for them. Amy was shoved roughly down into a chair. The handcuffs at her back rubbed against her wrists; they were tearing the skin and causing bleeding. She made a note that if she ever tried handcuffs with James, they would be fur-lined.

Her uncle barked out another order which made Amy jump. Leon came back around to Amy's side, and the gun pointed at her temple again.

"Now I have your full attention, Mr North? After your wilful attempts at escape, I now have funeral costs and medical bills to cover. I think I will have to increase the amount that I require from you. And I would suggest you waste no more time in trying to delay the inevitable. I want £20 million in my account in the next half hour. Or," he pointed toward Leon, "I will let you watch as my associate here take whatever he wants from my niece. And believe me, he has some very peculiar tastes that tend to leave his ladies a little broken." Leon cracked his knuckles in Amy's ear, and she felt sick again.

"Get me my phone. I will show you how to transfer the money to whatever account you want. It will be done in moments." Amy knew the tone in James' voice, he was just waiting for what he now saw as the inevitable. His death or Amy's. Her uncle sent the only other guard in the room that was conscious to get James' phone. While they waited, her uncle strode up to Amy and patted her cheek,

"So naive, so pretty. Such a waste. You were too much like him." Amy turned her head away, she didn't want to be touched by this man, she wanted him to rot in hell. He pulled it back and gripped her tightly by the chin. "You know; you are just like your whore of a mother. She was always playing hard to get, but the reality was; she loved it rough."

The moment of clarity that Amy needed hit. Her uncle had fancied her mother, but she had chosen her father. She had her advantage and she was damn well going to use it.

"I am surprised you wanted me around if you felt that badly towards my mother. After all, everyone always said I was the spitting image of her when she was my age. Were you trying to make me into the whore you thought she was?"

He laughed out loud and pulled her towards him and

away from Leon. Leon stepped to the side and pointed his gun at James' head. James still stood silent and in his own world.

"Your mother *was* a whore, Amy. How do you think we met her? She was one of the girls at the club. Entrapped your fucking father with her feminine ways. Got him to marry her, the money-grabbing bitch. She went for the brother with the bigger share of the fortune."

"You know that is not true. She wanted nothing to do with this place. It is why we moved out to Essex."

"No, you moved because nobody would accept she was the boss. And she sweet talked your father into giving up his business and his blood family."

"You don't mean that."

"Yes I do Amy."

Amy screamed at him now, "You agreed to their marriage. You gave your blessing. You were my dad's best man."

"You think I had a choice? Your dad had all the control. I did what he wanted, or I was out. Your mum had him wound around her little finger so tightly that he didn't know the truth from reality anymore."

"That is complete bullshit."

"For fuck's sake Amy. Wake up. You know it is the truth."

Amy was struggling, she did know the truth, not the twisted version that her uncle had painted in his mind. She shut her eyes. She needed to calm this down. The fighting was making them both angrier, and it wasn't shaking James from his sorrows. She quietened her voice and forced the tears out of her eyes.

"We had a conversation about you one day. Mum and dad had had a big argument. He had stormed off out. She said she wondered what her life would have been like if she had married someone else. I asked her who, and she told me you."

"She would have been treated like a princess. She would

have been the centre of my world."

"I thought she was to my father. I guess I saw nothing that went on behind their closed bedroom door. It was all hidden from me."

The guard returned to the room with James' phone and handed it to her uncle.

"Amy, you know how your parents died don't you?"

"A car accident." They had skidded over the central reservation and into the path of a lorry coming the other way.

"The police report stated that it seemed as though they had been arguing. The cameras caught a heated discussion between them on the lead up to the point of the accident. The camera at the point of the crash showed your mother's hands, as well as your father's, on the wheel. It looked as though she had grabbed the wheel. She caused the accident, Amy. She was responsible for the death of my brother."

Amy turned her head away again and began to cry, this time, though, her pain was for real. James lifted his head. Was he coming back to her?

"No. No." She screamed the last no in desperate hopes it rang around James' head.

"I am sorry, Amy. It is the truth. I will show you the police reports if you want." Police reports, police reports... James had researched her, had he seen these reports? Had he kept the truth from her? Her heart was ripping; she could feel it tearing in two. Out of the corner of her eye, she saw Matthew move his hand. He had freed himself from the chains. She needed to get her hands free as well. She was no use as she was.

"Uncle Stephen, will you unchain me please? It doesn't have to be this way." She looked down at the phone. "I will ask James to help you out, he will do it for me. You have suffered as much as I have. My mother is at fault here. She killed my father and has destroyed us both." Her uncle hesitated. "Please. At least Dad left you the club. You can make it great without her interference. James could invest in it. We could do something great with it together. Please. It doesn't have to be this way. I want you in my life. You are the only family that I have."

The solemn expression on her uncle's face changed, the corners of his mouth curled upwards, and he began to laugh out loud. A cackle that made Amy jump, he grabbed her and shoved her to the floor.

"I want ten million pounds. And your fiancé over there is going to give it to me."

"What do you need money for? You own the club."

"I don't own this fucking club, Amy. You do. Your father left the whole thing to you in his will. And your lying, deceiving boyfriend, well he tried to sell it to me, without your knowledge. So you see Amy, you are just the same as your mother. A deluded little whore."

She opened her mouth to speak to James, but she noticed the expression on his face had changed. Gone was the defeat, and back was the murderous intent. This was something she could work with... but at what cost to their relationship?

CHAPTER TWENTY-SEVEN

James

The sound of Amy's anguished cry permeated the hazy fog that had become James' brain. She was suffering. He had to stop it; that was his duty to her. He looked up; she was bent over a table, and a man was on top of her. James lunged forward, but a gun was pointed at his head. He stilled.

He looked to see where Matthew was and got the sign from him that he was free and ready.

Amy had tears tumbling down her face. What was that man doing to her?

Amy looked at him. "Is that right?"

Her uncle turned.

James nodded. He needed to be honest. He couldn't lie now. He promised her he would never do that again.

Her uncle laughed, and James wanted to rip his stinking head from his body and feed it to the lions in Regent's Zoo.

"Just as I thought. You didn't even know that you owned the club. He never told you. God, Amy. I figured I was good keeping you in the dark. But your own lover? Is that how he made his millions? Stealing off his dumb blonde girl-friends?"

"I never lied to her."

"You never told me the truth, either." James stumbled backwards. Her eyes were full of daggers.

"You didn't need to know, Amy. You were away from the club. Matthew was keeping an eye on everything to en-sure that he didn't do any damage to your name. I was protecting you."

"Protecting or controlling, James?" Amy turned her head and pushed against Leon. "Will you let me up, creep? I am not here for you to rub your sad little erection all over." Amy's uncle nodded, and Leon reluctantly pulled her up. He didn't move too far from her, though. "So did I get any income out of this club I am supposed to own or have you both pocketed that for yourselves?"

"You got money, Amy. You really think a dancer earned what you got paid for pretty much doing nothing? You want to make money in this club, you have to give the clients a bit more special attention."

"Or you'd sell them to the highest bidder."

"You know I don't need any money you earn. I was letting your uncle keep everything. I just wanted your name away from the club. I wanted that man away from you."

"Is that not something that I had a right to decide for myself, James?" She turned to her uncle, "And as for you, if this truly is my club, then I guess you can knock the value off the money you want from James."

"You can't sell it."

"What? Why? I don't want it."

"It can't be sold until you are twenty-five, apparently. But I will get my solicitors to work on it, if that is what you want."

"Oh great. I am stuck with the local brothel. That is perfect. I can just see the headline news now. 'Billionaire's girlfriend is local Madame'. Sally Bridgewater will love that one." She turned her head to look at the guy behind her, "Will you stand back? I know you get your kicks from rubbing your tiny dick against women but I would rather you keep it to yourself."

James watched the man's face reddened, and then he grabbed Amy around the throat. James rushed forward, but Amy's uncle lunged straight for James and smacked him down on the table. Amy was thrust down next to him. They were millimetres from each other.

"Enough." Her uncle's voice came in a tone of finality. "I am getting rather bored. I want my money, now." He brought James' phone down on his face." And then this ends here. Mr North, transfer the money."

"One thing first." Amy struggled to get her words out.

"No, enough. The money."

"You are going to kill us the second you get the money, so let me die knowing this one final thing."

"What." Amy's uncle spat his answer at her.

"What was the date that I signed the papers?"

No, she didn't need to know that. "Amy, please."

"No, James. I want to know."

"How are you two supposed to be in love? You have done nothing but fight since you entered the room. Alright. I don't know the exact date, but it was when you were in India."

"India?" Amy looked into James' eyes, and he could see her heart breaking. He knew what was coming next. "Was it before or after we talked James?"

"Amy, please, if this is to be our final moments let's not do this."

"Before or after?" She was shaking and her demanding eyes bore into him.

"After."

James watched as she shut her eyes. She was breaking down before him, and he couldn't hold her. He wasn't sure she would let him anyway. "I love you, Amy. I only ever wanted you to be safe."

Amy kept her eyes shut and didn't answer him.

"Hey boss, while he transfers the money, can I show her what a real man can do to her?" James looked up and saw a malicious grin on the soon-to-be dead man's face if James could figure a way out of this.

"Go for it. It will provide some entertainment, and I bet it makes Mr North transfer the money a bit quicker. I wonder if she will scream as much as Sara did when we all took turns with her?"

James tried to struggle as he watched the man pull up Amy's skirt. He was too heavily pinned down. Was he really going to have to see her so utterly destroyed? Amy's uncle pulled him up and handed him the phone.

"Transfer the money now or I let him have a go, as well. I might even throw your mother in as well." He motioned towards the guard by Matthew and his mother.

Amy kicked back out at the man about to rape her and smacked him hard in the balls. Leon stumbled backwards and groaned loudly. Amy slid to the floor. Leon grabbed his gun and pointed it at her.

"Fucking bitch. You are dead."

A gunshot rang out, and a bright red dot of blood appeared on Leon's forehead. He gurgled and fell to the floor. James turned his head towards the direction of the shot and saw Sonia stumble into the room. She had a cut above her eye where she had obviously been attacked. She was swaying, so James guessed she had been knocked unconscious. From behind him came another groan of agony, Matthew, who had freed himself, sideswiped the guard with them, and ran him into the wall.

James, standing next to Amy's uncle, lashed out with his elbow and sent him flying to the floor. James launched himself round the table and grabbed Amy. He needed to check she was alright. He pulled back the hair that was over her face. She had dried blood on her mouth.

"Amy, Amy. Look at me."

"Is it over?"

"Yes, beautiful. You won't be hurt now."

"James." The panicked call from Matthew came from behind him. James saw the gun on the table. He grabbed it and spun around. Amy's uncle had gotten to his feet and pointed a gun at them.

"What were you saying about this being over?"

James followed the trajectory of the gun's aim straight to Amy. James pulled back the trigger. Falling sideways as he shot, he pushed Amy out of the way. His shot hit her uncle and ripped through his chest. The old man stumbled forward, dropping his gun. Matthew tackled him to the ground. Blood frothed at Amy's uncle's mouth.

James suddenly registered a searing agony from his side. He clutched it as he landed on the floor and rolled onto his back. A crack came from the other side of the table as Matthew broke Amy's uncle's neck. James could barely register it, though. His head was spinning, and everything was turning cloudy. The pain in his side was travelling and burning. He pulled his hand away from the pain and held it up. It was covered in blood. He could hear Amy hysterically screaming and screaming. Matthew appeared at his side and placed his hand hard onto where it was hurting him. His head started spinning more as he heard calls for an ambulance. All the time everything was blackening, Amy came to his ear and was pleading, she was pleading for him to hold on, to live. He tried to answer her but nothing came out. The pain was so intense he couldn't take it anymore. Darkness enclosed him and everything went silent.

CHAPTER TWENTY-EIGHT

Amy

The ambulance seemed to take an age to weave through the London traffic. Amy wanted to scream at everyone to get out of their way, but instead she stayed silent and watched the paramedic work on James. He was pale because he had lost a lot of blood. Amy's hands were stained with it. His top had been ripped away, and all these things stuck to his chest. Machines beeped around him, but James just lay there silent. He had not regained consciousness. As they pulled into the A&E emergency bay, the ambulance doors were flung open, and the bed James was in wheeled out. Doctors crowded around him and began to discuss his vital statistics. She felt so helpless. She just wanted to make him better, but she had to let the doctors do their job. All she could do was pray.

James was wheeled straight into the resuscitation room. Amy was stopped at the door, and she stood there as they closed on her. She was still crying, her mouth hurt and her head as well. She was shaking. What did she do now? How long before she could see him again? What were they doing in there? Why couldn't she be in there with him? Did he know she wasn't there? Was he upset?

A nurse came over to her and put a hand on her shoulder, Amy jumped.

"Miss Jones is it? Please, I won't hurt you."

Amy sobbed.

"Please come this way, I have a room you can wait in." Amy suddenly became aware of the faces of those waiting to be seen all watching her. The nurse again placed her hand around Amy to guide her. "I will get you a nice cup of tea as well. You look like you need one. I think some ice for that lip as well. We should get a doctor to check that bump on your head."

Amy allowed herself to be directed to a room. She was numb. "What are they doing to him?"

"They're trying to stabilise him. His blood pressure fell in the ambulance, and his heartbeat is erratic. They're worried about the damage the bullet did."

"Will he be alright?"

"Honey, I am going to be honest with you. I don't know. We need to just let the doctors do their thing."

Amy let out a shuddering breath as she nodded acceptance of what the nurse was saying. The nurse helped her to sit. The room smelt of cleaning fluid, the whole place did. The fact she was in a hospital was beginning to sink in, everything still seems so scattered in her brain. The gunshots were still ringing in her head.

"Thank you."

"I will get you that tea, and I will get a doctor to come and look at you here as well. You may need a CAT scan on that bump, but we will see what he says."

Amy turned away and just looked at the door, her right hand was rubbing over the diamond of her engagement ring on her left. She felt like she was in a nightmare. It was hard to even process everything that had just happened.

She felt like it had been days since she had slept. It probably was actually. They had left the Maldives early in the morning, and the flight had been a long one.

A doctor returned with the nurse and Amy's cup of tea. He examined Amy and asked her loads of questions. She may have answered them correctly, she may not have. She really didn't know, but he seemed satisfied and said that as she hadn't blacked out, she could be observed while they waited for news of Mr North. The door suddenly flung open; Matthew, Miranda and Sonia entered the room. The doctor immediately went to Sonia, who was virtually being carried by Matthew as she still seemed so dizzy. The doctor demanded she be admitted straight away and sent for a scan so the nurse and the doctor hurried away with her. Matthew tried to go with her, but Sonia demanded he stayed with Amy. Matthew did as he was told. Another nurse came and took Miranda for examination. This left just Amy and Matthew alone in the waiting room.

"Have they said anything?"

"They're stabilising him. We are to wait."

"I hate these places."

Amy turned her head to look at him. Her eyelids were heavy.

"I suppose, in your line of work, it is one place you never want to see."

"Yeah. Means we have failed in our duty."

"You didn't fail. It was an intense situation."

"He will be alright. It is probably just the blood loss causing the trouble."

"Are you always this casual afterwards?"

"After what?"

"Killing someone?"

"Your uncle?"

Amy swallowed and met Matthew's eyes for the first time. They were red-rimmed, and he looked tired. She saw in that instance that nothing he had just done was easy for him. "I am sorry. He deserved it."

"Nobody deserves death, Amy. I don't make the decision to take someone's life lightly. I ended your uncle's life because he was dying. James' shot may have hit the mark, but it wasn't going to be a quick death. Snapping his neck ended it with less pain and fear."

"You should have let him suffer. He wouldn't have done the same for you."

"You don't mean that."

"Don't I?"

"No, you have an amazingly kind heart, and you saved James. He was on a path to total destruction, but your love and perseverance with him have made him an entirely different man."

"You really think that?"

"I do."

"So why did he lie to me?"

"Because he loves you and wanted to protect you from what you were too naive to understand."

"Naive." Amy got to her feet and walked to the small window, she leant against the frame, it was cold to touch and made her shiver slightly. "So you think I am a child as well."

"No. I don't. I believe you are wiser than you give yourself credit for. I do, however, think you choose not to see things. You worked in a brothel for a year, Amy, you must have known what went on? What about signing stuff for the club? Did you never have to sign anything for your uncle?"

She turned back to face him.

"You are right. I knew what went on, I chose to believe the best of my uncle. I wasn't forced to do it so I ignored it. And there were times I signed things, I never read them. I always believed what he told me. I trusted him. Just the same as I trusted James."

"Amy, this was never malicious on James' part. I promise you. He just wanted to protect you from being hurt. He hated seeing you in pain. The night in the club when he had to show you that video. It killed him. I saw him punishing himself that day and every day afterwards until you forgave him. You are his world."

"You know, if he had told me I would have told him to sell the club. I don't want that sort of place."

"I know. I think he knows that as well." Amy looked down at her engagement ring again. So much had happened in such a short space of time. And she didn't just mean the events of the day. She had only known James for a few months. She felt like she was drowning in it all. "What are you going to do?" Matthew got up from his chair and came over to her. He touched the engagement ring.

"I don't know." She loved James so much. But it was as if everything was too intense. It was all just coming one thing after another. She needed to slow it down. She needed to find her own pace and even her own breath again.

Matthew brought her into his arms and comforted her, it was the first time since her father had died that she felt like she was being watched over with a familial warmth. She mumbled into Matthew's jacket.

"Can I ask you something?" She brought her head up so she could see his reaction. "What my uncle said about the way my parents died. Do you know if it was true?"

He sighed.

"I have seen the police reports, Amy. There was no indication they were fighting. I spoke to an associate of mine about the accident." He paused. "All indications pointed to the fact that your uncle had them murdered. But it could not be proved. Amy, your mum was never supposed to be in that car. The meeting they were heading to was just supposed to be between your uncle and your father. It was meant to be about your father selling his half of the club to your uncle. She didn't want him to go through that alone, it would seem, and joined him. They died together, very much in love."

Amy went silent, she couldn't speak. Her brain was unable to process any more information.

The door opened, and a doctor came in,

"Miss Jones?"

"How is he?" Amy jumped to her feet.

"He is stable and awake. We have moved him to a private room. He is asking for you."

"Oh, thank god." Amy brought her still-bloody hands to her face to stifle the relieved sobs.

"I will take you to him now if you wish?"

"Yes, please." Amy turned back to Matthew, "Thank you. You should go find Miranda and tell her. Go be with Sonia afterwards. She needs you."

"I will."

Amy nodded at him and then followed the doctor to where James was.

The room was sterile and cold, machines surrounded James and beeped in time with his heart beat. He had a drip in his arm and another one feeding blood into him. He still looked pale as he lay there in the bed. He had his eyes shut but as soon as she closed the door he opened them and looked at her.

"Amy." His voice was croaky and weak.

"I am here." She came beside the bed and took his hand.

"I love you."

"I love you, too." Her voice broke.

"What happened?"

"We are all safe. My uncle...he is dead." James groaned and shut his eyes again. "Your mum will be here soon. A nurse took her to ensure she was well."

"I am sorry."

"You need to rest. Now isn't the time to talk. Get some sleep. I will go home and change, then come back and sit with you."

"Don't leave me."

Please. I am covered in blood. I need a shower."

"I shouldn't have got you to sign that paper."

"James, not now." Her voice was breaking.

"I need to know you forgive me. Please."

Amy pulled her hand away from his and turned away. She couldn't do this now. Everything was still so confusing.

"James, I am going to go and change."

"Don't walk out on me." His tone was pleading but also had the air of control in it.

"James, please."

"Look at me."

Her body betrayed her, and she turned around. "I can't, I can't do this now."

"Tell me that you forgive me for what I did. I won't do it again. You have my word. I will change. I love you so much."

Amy brought her hands up to her face and covered her eyes as she began to shake her head. "Oh god, I am so confused." She was shaking.

"You need to sleep. Everything will be better tomorrow. I will come home. We can go to my country estate for a while and rest. I think I will need some time to recover from this."

"No."

"We just need time. Everything has been a big shock. You have been through so much today."

"No. It isn't that." She looked down at her engagement ring and took it off her finger. She placed it on his chest, tears now streaming down her face.

"Stop it. Don't be silly. Come here and put your ring back on. You are not going to do this." The machine next to him started beeping as his heart rate accelerated.

Amy leant over the bed and kissed his lips. He tried to move his arms to pull her back to stay with him, but he was sluggish from all the drugs and she evaded him.

"Lanzarote, James. Lanzarote."

Finally, a Happily Ever After

6 months later.

"You need to point your toes when you spin to the left. It makes the movement seem more fluid. Like you are water flowing over the floor. Roll your arms more from the wrists as well."

"Like this, Miss?"

"A little bit more. Feel the music, become lost in it. Shut your eyes, listen to the beat."

The sixteen-year-old private student performed the move again, this time perfectly.

"Yes, yes just like that."

She jumped for joy, and Amy stepped back proudly. She had been working with her for a couple of months now in preparation for her audition at a dance academy. It was fantastic to see the way she was developing, and Amy was sure that she would easily pass the test.

"Well done Emily. We are done for the day. Go home and get some rest. Feet up. Lots of carbohydrates. You will need it for tomorrow. You will do brilliantly, though. I can feel it. Break a leg." Amy and Emily both giggled.

"Thank you, Miss Amy. You have been so wonderful. I will text you tomorrow to let you know how it went."

"Please do. I will be anxious until I hear."

It had been two months since Amy had opened the dance school. It had taken about four months to convert the club into the school. She had to redecorate and disinfect so many of the rooms, although the dark room at the back was sealed up. She never went in there. Some of the smaller rooms had been rented out to music teachers and for after-school clubs. She had kept the stage area as it was to rent out to local groups who wanted it for their own performances. She would also plan an end of term display for all her students as well.

Amy had worked night and day on this project. It was all she had left. It hadn't been easy. People knew what the club had once been. They knew about the deaths that occurred there, and it took a lot of word of mouth and advertising just to get people in the door. She was sleeping in one of the back rooms so that she was still able to rent out her flat and use the income to put into the school. Her uncle's patrons hadn't taken kindly to the change either. And she had to pay out a lot in redundancy to the previous employees of the club. It hadn't been easy. At first, she had thrown herself into the work just to stop crying. She was utterly destroyed by the events of the day James had been shot. She tried not to think of him, but he always seemed to come into her mind when she least expected it, and she would break down. Elena had tried to get her to go to clubs with her and her friends or even just down the pub for a drink, but Amy wasn't ready. She said she had lost all her confidence, but the reality was she was still very much in love with James. She had seen him on the news and in newspapers. He was busy working on his hotels. A few weeks ago he had been photographed out clubbing with two girls, and the heading stated he was back on the market after having his heart broken and was certainly enjoying himself. Amy hadn't even gotten out of bed that day. She couldn't face it. He had moved on; Amy was his past. She was the one who had walked out on him.

"How did Emily do?" Elena interrupted Amy's thoughts.

"She did well. I think she is finally ready. She will ace the audition."

"Brilliant. You should really start doing your teaching exams. You are a natural dancer. You don't need me apart from the qualified bit."

"You want to leave me already?" Amy looked sadly at

her friend.

"Well no, just saying." Elena came and gave Amy a big cuddle. They hadn't known each other for long, but they had definitely become close. "Right. I am not going to take no for an answer today. I am going out tonight dancing, and you are coming with me."

"Lena, no."

"No arguments Amy. You are twenty-one, and you need to live more. Come on let's get you some clothes to wear."

Elena dragged Amy through the club to the room that was used for a bedroom. She opened the small wardrobe Amy had and sighed.

"Is that it? You have like three outfits."

Amy had walked out of James' life with nothing. She had her bank account card and the clothes she'd had on but they were covered in blood. She hadn't felt right taking all the stuff he had bought for her. Clothes hadn't been a priority.

"Sorry. I will just put my PJ's on and relax in front of the TV instead."

"No, you won't. You can come to my house. We are a similar size--you can wear something of mine."

"El..."

Amy began but didn't get to finish before she was dragged from the room and towards the doors of the club. Part of her wanted to run back and lock herself in her bedroom, but another part knew she had to begin living again. The latter part won and she allowed herself to be led out for the evening.

Fours hour later, Amy and Elena were in the night club and on their second drinks. Elena's mates were friendly, and Amy was actually enjoying herself. She felt a bit over-done--her hair had been pulled and twisted into an elaborate style, she had more makeup on than she usually wore, and the skirt Elena had chosen for her... well Amy knew she wouldn't be bending over in it anytime tonight. Not if she didn't want the whole club to see her backside.

Elena downed a Jägerbomb. "Come on Amy, let's show

these people how you actually dance to this."

Amy looked at Elena's friends, "Is she always this excitable in a club?"

They all nodded in unison. A brunette who was called Samantha shouted over the music,

"She downs the drinks and then dances them off. Never gets a hangover."

"Unlike you, Sammy."

"True, but then I look like a grandma when I dance."

They all laughed again.

"Come on Amy, please."

"Alright. I am coming. But if I break my ankle in your sky high shoes then you will have to take all my classes for a month."

"You won't." Elena started to groove with the music as they both headed to the dance floor and began to perform a bit of a routine to the song. People around them started clapping. The tune finished, and Elena drifted off into her own world as the next one came on. Amy did the same. It was a bit slower in rhythm and allowed her to sway her hips and pretty much dance like she used to in the club. She became lost in the music.

For the first time in months she was happy and relaxed. She was glad she had allowed Elena to bring her here. From behind her, a pair of masculine hands slid around her hips. She turned to look at the guy. He was cute. She smiled and slowed her rhythmic movement of her hips in time with his. She was single, even if she didn't feel like it. She might as well enjoy herself.

His hands gripped tighter as she gyrated against him, one song flowed into another and Amy became lost in the freedom of the beat.

Then she heard a voice which sent shivers down her spine.

"Get your fucking hands off her."

She swung round to see James grab the guy that she was dancing with and pull him off her. The guy pushed James back.

"Get lost, loser."

Amy saw the flash of rage on James' face. She jumped between them and pressed her hand against James' broad chest. Her betraying body sparked with energy from his closeness.

"Go away, James."

"Yeah, do as you're told buddy. Wait your turn. I am going to fuck her first."

Amy registered his words with shock. She saw James clench his fist but gave him a look and turned back to the now not-so-cute guy.

"What did you say?"

"Come on babe? You are so gagging for it. You can do him after if he hasn't found anyone else."

"You think I am going to sleep with you?"

"Nobody dances like that who isn't asking for my rock hard cock inside them."

People around them began to give them some space as they sensed the tension.

"Please can I, Amy?" James spoke from behind her.

"You are asking my permission for something?"

"I know, and I have only had one beer."

"Only one. You must be getting old. Be my guest, James."

And with that, Amy turned on her heel and left the dance floor. Elena stopped her,

"Is that *the* James?"

"Yes, it is. Elena, I have had a good night, but I am going to grab a taxi home. I will catch you tomorrow."

"I will come with you."

"No, you stay and enjoy yourself. I will text you when I am home."

"If you are sure."

"I am."

Amy hugged her friend just as the sounds of a fight broke out behind them. Matthew appeared in front of Amy.

"I left him for one minute."

"Sorry, Matthew."

"No worries Miss Jones, it is my job."

Matthew sped past her and into the fight as Amy headed out into the fresh air. So much for a new start.

COMING SOON...Divided Control

Six months after her split from James, Amy has changed the club beyond all recognition and it is now a dance school. She has achieved something for herself at last but is she living or is she fooling herself that she shouldn't have used her safe word.

James has recovered from the physical injuries of that night but has he learnt his lesson about the irrepressible need to control. He may have done it for the right reasons, but Amy is not an ordinary girl, she won't lay down and be his submissive 24/7.

Divided Control is the sequel to Surrendered Control; it takes you on the next part of Amy and James' journey. Though a holiday to Las Vegas and a visit to a BDSM club, a trip to Yorkshire for a wedding and a figure James' had hoped to keep away from his family returning; Divided Control will take you on a wild journey and test your emotions to the maximum.

Are you ready to step into the world of Control?

About Anna Edwards

This is the first novel from Anna Edwards, she is a British Author that has a love of travelling and developing plot lines for stories. She has spent that last two years learning the skills of writing after being an Accountant since the age of 21. As well as Roleplaying on twitter, she can also be found writing poetry.

This novel combines two of her favourite travel destinations to give an international feel to her romance. Lanzarote is a popular holiday destination for the writer, many a summer has been spent in Playa Blanca sampling the food and the sun. India is a place that she lived for eighteen months with her husband and two children. Her young son was only six months when she travelled out there. It was a fabulous time for the family and they learnt so much about the differing cultures, as well as spending lots of money in the silk shops.

Connect with Anna Edwards:
www.AuthorAnnaEdwards.com
Facebook Page: AnnaEdwardsWriter
Facebook Profile: Anna Edwards
Twitter: @Anna__Edwards
Instagram: anna__edwards

21714179R00111

Printed in Great Britain
by Amazon